I0684316

With Violent Hands: Youths and Murder in 1945 Britain

By

Conrad Lisk

Edited by Winston Forde

With Violent Hands

Published by SONDIATA GLOBAL MEDIA Ltd
(Songlome)

First Edition

SONDIATA GLOBAL MEDIA
WE MUST ON OUR NARRATIVE

ISBN-13:978-1-9997878-6-8
**Cover image Adapted by Sondiata Global Me-
dia Ltd**
http://www.sondiataglobalmedia.com

Songlome
36 Luna Road, Surrey CR7 8NY UK

Dedication

To my dear mother, Rachel Joya Lisk, who passed away while I was finalising this work.

Also to the following who feature within these pages:

Ivy May Phillips (1918 – 1945)

Gerhart Rettig (1919 – 1945)

And

James Parker Denike (1926 – 1944)

Acknowledgments

Thanks to all those who assisted in the creation of this work. Once again, thanks to my parents for giving me an enduring interest in history. Also to my wife and daughter for putting up with the amount of time I spend researching and writing. Thanks particularly to the relatives of people involved in the cases contained in this book – particularly Marco Mundhenk and Gillian Bulstrode – for all the help they provided. Thanks also to Emma Crutchley for taking photographs in the German War Graves at Cannock Chase. Many thanks to Squadron Leader Winston Forde RAF (Retired) for all his work in editing this book.

[Cover photograph: A Browning Hi-Power automatic (US Bureau of Alcohol, Tobacco and Firearms)]

With Violent Hands

'With violent hands a young man tried

To mend the shape of life.

This one used a shotgun

And that one used a knife.

And who can see our issues plain

That vex our groaning dust?

"The law is greater than the man,"

Says Harry Fat the just.

Te Whiu was too young to vote,

The prison records show.

Some thought he was too young to hang;

Legality said *No*.

Who knows what fear the raupo hides

Or where the wild duck flies?

"A trapdoor and a rope is best,"

Says Harry Fat the wise.'

A Rope For Harry Fat, by James Keir Baxter.

Contents

Introduction

This is the story of a crime and its aftermath. The tragedy which starts this story occurred in Britain towards the end of the Second World War. It was, of course, a very different world then from now.

We will go through the investigation of the offence, and the arrest and trial of the perpetrator. The book will examine some quirks of the then-existing law of murder. The events described took place at a time when almost all persons convicted of murder in England and Wales were sentenced to death by hanging. We shall see to what extent these sentences were carried out, and how decisions were made as to which convicts lived or died. The book will also look at the way the criminal justice system dealt with prisoners at that time.

In addition to looking at the civilian justice system, the book also looks at a parallel case which went through the military justice system at much the same time. We will also follow those participants who survived the events, to see what happened to them subsequently.

Chapter One: Tragedy At The Garage

June 1945. Britain was exhausted after almost six years of war. She was partly victorious, but also still fighting. Germany, which had started the war in 1939, had surrendered at the beginning of May. However Japan, which had been fighting Britain, the US and the other Western Allies since late 1941, had not given in. While many British and other Allied service personnel based in France, Belgium and Germany were coming home on leave or permanently, others were not so fortunate. Tens of thousands of their comrades-in-arms remained in the Far East, fighting the Japanese. Many more were there as prisoners of the enemy, kept in horrific conditions.On Britain's streets, much remained the same as during the war in Europe. Much of the rubble left by air raids and more recent flying bomb attacks was still there. However, the nightly 'blackouts' enforced to discourage air raids were at an end. The tape put on windows to limit the effect of blasts was coming down. Rationing was still in force, and would be for years to come. The shadow economy, dominated by 'spivs', was very much in evidence, with many people buying 'black market' goods stolen or otherwise acquired outside the rationing system. This all contributed to an overall increase in crime during the war.[1]

Wartime crime is nowadays generally associated with 'loveable rogue' characters like Private Walker, the 'spiv' in the 'Dad's Army' TV comedy series in the 1960s/1970s. However, violent crime had continued throughout the conflict. Much of it capitalised on the chaos and disruption caused by air raids and the blackout. Gordon Cummins, an RAF cadet, murdered four women during a six-day spree during the Blitz in 1942. Likewise that April a man named Harry Dobkin was convicted of the murder the previous year of his estranged wife. He had buried her body in a church cellar hoping that she would be mistaken for an air-raid victim. Both men were hanged, Cummins's

---

[1] 10 facts about *Crime On The Home Front In The Second World War,* by Mark Ellis, BBC History Magazine, March 12 2018 online link.

execution taking place (appropriately enough) during an air raid.

Large numbers of American service-men came to the UK after the USA joined the war in 1941, creating upheavals which in some cases led to more crimes. The new-comers had access to coveted goods such as nylon stockings, chocolates and cigarettes, many of which made their way to the black market. The last months of 1944 led to a *cause celebre* featuring an American soldier. In October a US Army deserter, Karl Gustav Hulten, and a Welsh waitress, Elizabeth 'Betty' Jones, hijacked a London taxicab driven by George Heath. Hulten shot Heath dead. The US military allowed Hulten to be prosecuted, alongside Jones, by the British civilian authorities. The trial of the pair at the Old Bailey in January 1945 grabbed the headlines on both sides of the Atlantic. Both were convicted and sentenced to death. Eighteen-year-old Jones was fortunate to be 'reprieved' (that is, she was spared from the death penalty and imprisoned instead). Hulten, who was some four years older, was not so lucky. The crime was known as the 'Cleft Chin Murder' after the appearance of the victim[2].

At around 5.30pm 28 June 1945, Mrs Ivy May Phillips was cashing up at the Red Arrow Garage on Thornton Road, Thornton Heath, Croydon, where she worked as cashier and typist. The area was then occupied by a number of factories, and many workers were ending a shift at the time. The garage owner, Mr Ronald Samuel Booth, was working on his own car in the workshop while Ivy was in the office some ten yards away. At some stage, as Ronald related later, he heard a loud bang, and assumed that a compressor or a tyre must have exploded somewhere else on the premises. Initially he did not do anything, but then he heard shouting or screaming, presumably from the office. He ran towards there, and saw a man outside the office, 'disappearing' to the left, headed outside the garage. The man was wearing a fawn raincoat and a trilby hat.

Entering the office, he found Ivy lying on the floor. She was on her back with her

---

[2] The 1990 film *Chicago Joe and the Showgirl*, starring Emily Lloyd and Kiefer Sutherland, is based on this case.

knees up and her feet towards the door. Aubrey Frederick Cox ('Fred'), Ronald's foreman, entered the office behind him. Somewhat alarmingly Ronald then told Mr Cox to pursue the fleeing man: 'Go on Fred, he's just gone round the corner, go on and catch him.' Fred did as he was asked and gave chase.

Ronald knelt over Ivy, who was saying, over and over again, 'I've been shot.' Asked where, she replied 'In the stomach.' Ronald called 999, and went to make Ivy comfortable until an ambulance could arrive. Ronald asked Ivy 'if someone had tried to take her money,' and she responded 'I thought he was joking.' An ambulance soon arrived, and Ivy was taken to the nearby Mayday Hospital (now Croydon University Hospital).

Ronald was initially unsure how much money, if any, was missing. However it later turned out that about £5.00 had been taken.[3] The day was a Thursday, and therefore the next day was 'payday', albeit that the

---

[3] £1 then would be worth about £30 today.

wages to be paid would be weekly not monthly as would often be the case today. Had Ivy drawn out the money for wages, as was her usual practice, the robber may have escaped with much more, maybe as much as £30 to £50.

Ivy arrived at the Mayday Hospital and was admitted, and seen by a surgeon, a Mr Walsh, with a CID officer in attendance. She was operated upon and found to have a perforation in her liver and gut. She revived somewhat after the operation but the haemorrhage recurred.

The following morning, during a period of recovery, Ivy was questioned by Sergeant Whitelaw of the CID. This question and answer exchange took place:

Whitelaw: 'Can you tell me anything about the man who shot you? How old was he?'

Ivy: 'About 18 to 24 years.'

Whitelaw: 'How tall was he?'

Ivy: 'Medium, he was slim.'

Whitelaw: 'How was he dressed?'

Ivy: 'He had a brown felt hat.'

Whitelaw: 'Did he say anything?'

Ivy: 'Hand over money.' He showed me a bullet and said 'Look, I mean it.' He had a big black gun.

Whitelaw: 'Do you know the man?'

Ivy: 'He was a complete stranger.'

Whitelaw: 'How much money was there in the till?'

Ivy: '£5 in ten shilling notes [,] and £2 in silver in the desk.'

Returning to the time of the attack, Fred Cox had not been able to catch up with the assailant. He went all the way up Thornton Road to the main road, not seeing anyone running or acting suspiciously. Getting to the main London Road, he went to a police box, and called to report the shooting.[4] The call was put through to Norbury Police Station. Inspector Christmas and Sergeant Butcher of the CID promptly went by car to the garage, where they met Ronald at the office. Butcher found a cartridge of 5.5 calibre in the office. Inspector Albert Bastable of Croydon Police Station arrived on the scene later, and noticed holes in the paper blackout cover, and also in the shutter of the garage, indicating that the bullet had passed right through Ivy and out of the office, although the projectile itself was never found.

The police took statements almost immediately. It became clear that the private lives of Ronald and Ivy were somewhat complicated. In short, both were married but estranged, and at the time of the shooting had been in a live-in relationship with each other. Ronald gave a statement to Inspector Tasker of Croydon Police Station, which gave some detail of what had hap-

---

[4] These were large boxes carrying a telephone for use by police officers making calls to their station, or for members of the public wishing to call the police. They are probably most familiar to modern readers as the disguise of the TARDIS time machine in the TV science-fiction drama *Dr Who*.

pened. They had met in 1940, during the Blitz, when Ivy was working for the Civil Defence ambulance service and Ronald had been doing vehicle repairs for them.

Ivy had been born in London in 1917. Her mother, May Cole had been born in Gloucester in 1886, and the author has found no record of her ever having married. The name and occupation of Ivy's father are stated differently in various documents per taining to Ivy and her only sibling. He was 'John Herbert Johns' or 'John William Johns,' variously described as a builder or a 'maker of agricultural implements'. Ivy had married a chef, Edward Phillips in 1937.

Edward - born in 1918 - seems to have been a chef of some ability, as he is reported to have worked at West End hotels before the war. They had a son, John, in January 1939. Sadly, John Phillips passed away in April 1940, from bronchopneumonia. Ronald Booth had married in 1929, and had two sons, born in 1930 and 1933. Ronald was older than the Phillipses, having been born in 1903.

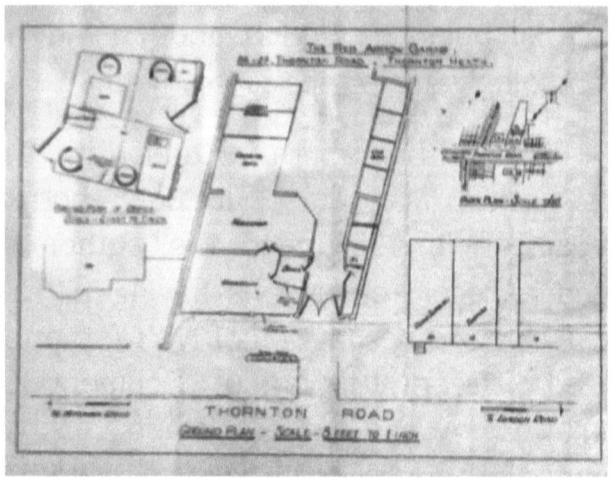

PC Cyril Weir's plan of the Red Arrow Garage and its surroundings, indicating the central location of the service bays and the office, at top left where the cartridge was found.

By the time Ronald and Ivy met, war had broken out and Edward was in the Royal Army Medical Corps, serving as a cook. At some stage their marriage failed. Ronald asserted in his 28 June statement that when he met Ivy 'relations between [the Phillipses] were not normal. They were friendly but each went their own way.' Ronald took Ivy out once or twice and they later began a relationship, eventually living together as man and wife in a flat at Tudor Close, Brixton.

By Ronald's account Edward did not find out about the relationship until about two years afterwards, and raised no objection. By then Ivy was working for Ronald as a supervisor in the Inspector Department, as he (Ronald) was sub-contracting to the Ministry for Aircraft Production. Ivy allegedly raised the possibility of divorce with Edward but nothing was done. Later, Ivy went back to the ambulance service, probably due to the 'Little Blitz' German air raids of early 1944 and the later rocket bomb attacks on London . However, she returned to work for Ronald in September 1944. A month or so before that, Edward had been posted abroad with the Allied forces in Europe, initially to France. When the war in Europe ended he was stationed at a British military hospital in Belgium. Despite the estrangement, the couple were in contact.

A few weeks before the shooting, Ivy had heard from Edward indicating that he was coming over to the UK on leave, apparently stating that he wanted to get things sorted out, although he did not expressly mention divorce. He arrived in London and visited Ivy at Tudor Close, when Ronald was not in, although he was aware of the meeting. Edward and Ivy had discussed divorce and arranged to meet in London later in the week, and did so. Edward did not state that he intended to remarry but it seemed implicit.

Ominously, Ronald related that Ivy had told him of Edward claiming to have a German Luger pistol and hundreds of rounds of ammunition. He also stated that the man he saw 'could have been Mr Phillips' but he could not say one way or another. Presumably the detective taking the statement thought that Edward would be the most likely suspect and was questioning Ronald accordingly. However Ronald also related that following the last meeting between the married couple, Edward had told Ivy he planned to return to his mother's house in Blackpool.

Had Ivy not remained conscious after the shooting, suspicion may have fallen on Edward. However as we have seen she would give an account that indicated an attacker unknown to her, and younger than her husband in any event. Thankfully his return to Blackpool was to provide him with an alibi. The Blackpool police received a phone call at 10.20pm on 28 June requesting them to locate Edward, which they did. Inspector Evans of the Blackpool Police Force went to Edward's mother's house at Cheltenham Road. Evans was swiftly satisfied that Ivy's husband could have had no involvement in her shooting. Edward had spent the evening with his parents, sister and four friends, at the South Pier show. He indicated that he would return to London to visit his injured wife.

Edward's own statement, taken down in Evans's notebook that night, tallies mostly with Ronald's. In it he related how he had come to England on 24 June, on ten days' leave. He had sent a telegram to Ivy on arrival at Dover, and phoned her when he had arrived at Victoria Station. He had visited her that night, no one else being with her in the flat. She had mentioned - this being the major difference between Ronald and Edward's accounts - that Ronald had said that he intended to go back to his wife and family, and that she did not know what she was going to do in future. On departing, Edward had told her that he would start divorce proceedings the following day, and asked for his bank book which had still been with her. She handed it over and they parted on good terms.

The following day, a Monday, he had gone to a firm of solicitors in Lincoln's Inn Fields, and started the process of obtaining a divorce. Later that day he met Ivy at Victoria Station and they had lunch together. He told her he had started the divorce proceedings. Ivy had left to bank some money from work. When they parted for the last time, they said 'Goodbye,' and Ivy had said, 'I don't suppose I will see you again.' Edward had said that it would probably not be advisable for them to communicate, (presumably owing to the legal proceedings) and that Ivy's army wife's allowance would be stopped as soon as Edward returned to base and informed his superiors of the pending divorce.

Edward, in his statement, speculated on whether Ivy would have been so depressed on the failure of her relationship with Ronald that she may have wanted to end her own life, and stated that he did not know whether she owned a pistol. He accepted that he himself owned a German Luger pistol with plenty of ammunition, but said that he did not have it with him – it was with his kit at the military hospital in Belgium. As in Ronald's statements, Edward indicated later that the two men seemed to have got on well, bearing in mind the awkward situation in which they found themselves. Edward was later to state that Ronald 'appeared to be fond of my wife.'

The easy-going rapport between the wife, her husband and her lover may be hard to understand even now. But this occurred against a background of changing morals during the war. It had perhaps always been accepted that when men went to war they would at some stage be unfaithful to their wives, fiancées or girlfriends. But this war had, for the first time, brought large-scale death and destruction to civilians at home during the Blitz and the later rocket-bomb attacks. Those at home, wo-men as well as men, also had the 'live for today' sentiment that soldiers and other service personnel had at the front. Many servicemen were surprisingly tolerant of their wives' affairs. It has been said that 'the strains of war were such that some women needed somebody –anybody –to comfort them in their loneliness, and the fact that they missed their absent husbands could make them more prone to tempta-tion, not less so.'[5] In his later statements Edward indicated that he had accepted his wife's admitted relationship with Ronald – he, Edward, being stationed in Scotland at the time. Ivy visited him there, frequently, often staying locally for a while. However when she informed him on one of these vis-its that she was now living with Ronald as man and wife Edward responded that in that case, he wanted nothing more to do with her. But they still parted on friendly terms at the end of that visit. Edward had not yet told his superiors of the split, thus leaving his wife in receipt of an army wife's allowance.

---

[5] Reader's Digest, *Yesterday's Britain*, 1998, p155.

Meanwhile the story of the garage shooting had hit the papers. Lurid stories dominated the headlines. The day after the robbery, the *Star* gave an amazingly detailed account of the robbery, under the headline 'Shot Woman: London Hunt For Gunman'. According to them, Superintendent Fred Cherrill, the Scotland Yard fingerprint expert, was called out of a theatre to help the local police in their investigation. The article also claimed, citing no source, that the robber had said to Ivy 'Stick them up and don't make a move,' while pointing the gun at her and moving towards the till. Allegedly as Mrs Phillips had stepped forward to stop him opening the drawer, he had fired at her and she had fallen. The robber had grabbed a few notes and left. The article concluded by stating that 'Cafés in the West End and other premises were visited at intervals throughout the night.' That article described the gunman as Ronald had – five feet six inches (167 centimetres), aged about 30, wearing a light fawn raincoat and a soft hat. Ivy was reported to be 'progressing satisfactorily.'

The following day, the papers reported Ivy's police interview on the 29th. The *Daily Mail* reported that 'dozens of photographs of dangerous criminals' had been taken to the Mayday Hospital for Ivy to look at. The article also reported that the police had amended the description of the suspect based on Ivy's statement – they were now looking for a man aged about 24, of medium height, slim build with dark brown hair. According to the article Ivy's condition was still serious.

This, sadly was true. Despite her periods of consciousness and responses to questioning, the operation of the 28th June had not been a success. A second operation had been carried out on 29th June. Ivy's condition improved briefly, but she passed away at 7.30 on the morning of the 30th June. Her brother H____, a Post Office telephone engineer, identified the body. A post-mortem was carried out the following day by pathologist Dr David Haler, with the liver injury being found to be the cause of death.

The search for the robber thus became a murder hunt. The *Sunday Dispatch* for 1 July 1945, ran the headline 'Hunt For A Slim Murderer With A Big Nose.'

Predictably, the police received lots of irrelevant information leading them to chase a number of leads. Somehow the London police ended up interrogating two Liverpool men detained in the latter city in connection with the robbery. In addition, the Colchester police took a statement from a Newfoundland gunner detained in the town's military detention centre (the famous 'glasshouse') about his possession of a firearm, which was seen as linked to the Liverpool suspects. As we have seen from Edward's situation, the aftermath of the war had left many soldiers in possession of firearms which had originally been seized as trophies by combat soldiers, but later sold, given or gambled away, often to soldiers in non-combatant trades. The *Daily Mail*, on 3 July 1945, duly reported the detention of the Liverpool suspects. It also reported the finding of a Luger pistol in a building in the Strand, in central London. The paper wrongly reported that this was the gun used in the shooting.

Late on 29 June a business traveller gave a lift to a man near Leeds, and reported this encounter the next day to the police as they felt the hitch hiker's description tallied with that of the wanted man. On July 2, a commuter made a statement to the police stating that on that day he had been on a train between London Paddington and Caversham and noted that a man on the train in railway company uniform had been carrying a firearm tucked into his inner right breast pocket. The alleged suspect was wearing the uniform of a driver or of a train 'fireman' or engine worker.

In the event none of these leads would result in any progress. The truth lay much closer to Thornton Heath.

Chapter Two: The House at Luxor Street

The breakthrough came unexpectedly on the night of 2 July. A young man who gave his name as Donald Raycaston met two police officers in a street in Camberwell, South London. There is little information on his appearance except that Inspector Bastable was later to describe him as having the unhealthy look of a tuberculosis sufferer. Donald told the officers that he knew where the gun used in the Thornton Heath shooting was – it was at a house in Luxor Street, Camberwell where he, Donald, lived. In circumstances which would be highly irregular now, the police officers simply asked Donald to recover the gun. He did so, bringing a large automatic pistol wrapped in rags to Camberwell police station – a 9mm Browning automatic. The policemen got Donald to make a statement to a detective sergeant, which contained the account stated below.

According to Donald, he was then working as a lorry driver employed by a firm in Camberwell. Up to the first week in May

1945, he had been living in Foreign Street, also in Camberwell. However, on the night of V-E Day, 8 May 1945 – a night of wild celebrations as the country marked the end of the war in Europe – Donald met another young man called Peter Jarmain (although Raycaston in his initial statements gave the family name as 'Jarman.'). Donald was about twenty, Peter was eighteen. Donald was later to state that he had previously known Peter, but neither man ever seems to have mentioned when or where they might have met before. As a result of this meeting Donald left Foreign Street and moved in to lodge with Peter's family.

They lived in a house at nearby Luxor Street. The family was made up of Peter, his young brother R____, aged thirteen, who had just returned from evacuation following the end of the risk of rocket bomb attacks, and Peter's mother. His father had passed away a few years previously. There were three other siblings. Two siblings were in the services, - a brother, Sydney, serving in Germany with the Royal Engineers, and an older sister, Betty, serving with the WAAF (the female branch of the Air Force) elsewhere in England. A younger sister, D_____, aged about sixteen also did not live in the house.

According to Donald, he and Peter initially socialised together. However, Peter soon fell in with a group of lads who he started to go out with, and Donald had, in his words 'given Peter up.' Donald described Peter as five feet eight inches (172 centimetres) tall, and a stylish dresser, with a thin moustache.

Donald told how on the day of the shooting[6] he had been in a pub, the Wickwood Tavern at Flaxman Road, Camberwell, at between 9 and 10pm. (The pub was just a few minutes' walk from Luxor Street and was probably his 'local.') He had been with his girlfriend and her father. Peter and two others had entered the pub – a soldier called Leonard ('Lennie') Dunn, who Donald said he knew slightly, and another man who Donald did not know. Peter had asked to speak to Donald privately. When they were alone, Peter asked Donald if he had

---

[6] Most likely he was in error as we shall see later, this probably happened on the following day, the Friday.

read in the papers about 'the Thornton Heath job,' Donald replied yes. Peter then claimed that he had 'done it.' Donald refused to believe this, and called Peter a liar. Peter then went on to ask Donald for a loan of five pounds to pay the person who had sold him the gun - he had referred to the firearm as a 'rod', using slang then current in pulp crime novels and in gangster movies. Donald said that he did not have the money, but might get it by the weekend.

The two young men did not meet for a couple of days. On the Sunday night, Donald was in the pub again, and Peter walked in. He said to Donald 'I've got something to show you when you get indoors.' He then left the pub accompanied by Dunn and the other person. On getting back to Luxor Street more than an hour later, Donald went in to the kitchen on the basement floor. Peter followed him in holding something wrapped up in a rag – he removed the rag to reveal an automatic pistol. Donald took it from him and asked 'Is this thing loaded?' Peter did not reply, but took the clip out of the gun, showing that it had bullets in it.

Placing the clip on the table, Peter had gone on to state how he had shot Ivy.

"He pulled the breech back and a bullet fell out. It had not been fired. He then let the breech back and said 'a bullet has automatically gone into the breech'[....] . He said, 'I went in there and the lady was counting the money. I said "I'll have that, sister," and she said "Don't be silly."' Continuing, he said 'I changed the gun from my right hand to my left to take the money with my right hand, and as I did so, the gun went off and the lady fell down groaning. I picked the money up, and ran out and got on a 'bus.'"

Donald said 'You have been a silly little bugger,' and took the gun from him. He later left with it, taking it to his girlfriend's address, leaving Peter at home with Dunn who had been in the living room. Donald showed the gun to his girlfriend's father, and explained what had happened. Donald said that he intended to take the gun to the police station, but the father advised him not to as he might get into further trouble. Donald went back to Luxor Street with the firearm. He gave it back to Peter who asked why Donald had returned it. Donald asked him to put it away, and said that he would try to get the money by 2nd July. Donald later saw Peter put the gun, wrapped up once more, up the chimney of the fireplace.

Earlier on the night of his encounter with the police, Donald left Peter at Luxor Street and went out to meet his girlfriend. She and her parents advised Donald to tell the police what he knew. He left, and on his way home met the two policemen. After the discussion with them, already referred to, Donald went back to Luxor Street and retrieved the firearm without Peter or anyone else noticing.

Sergeant Himus, who had taken Donald's statement, contacted Inspector Bastable about the new development. On Bastable's instructions, Donald was brought from Camberwell to Croydon Police Station, together with the gun. (Presumably he was taken by car as it is some eight miles' distance.) On hearing of Donald's account, Bastable noted that Lennie Dunn, Peter's soldier friend, was on the list of former garage employees given by Ronald. Donald stated that Peter knew about the garage as Lennie had worked there.

Bastable then went to Luxor Street, along with Donald, Inspector Tasker and Sergeant Himus. The officers sent Donald in to check that Peter was in. He returned to say that Peter was in bed in a room on the ground floor. It is not clear where Donald went after this but he may have gone back to Camberwell Police Station later. Bastable and Inspector Tasker entered the house, apparently using a key tied to a piece of string attached to the front door.

In a room on the ground floor they found Peter and his young brother asleep in one bed. There was another empty bed in that room, Donald's. Bastable woke Peter up, told him that they were police officers making enquiries into the garage shooting, and that they thought he could assist. Peter replied, 'I know the garage but I cannot help you with the murder. I know nothing about it.' Bastable stated that they wanted Peter to give them an account of his movements on the day of the murder.

Peter agreed, and got dressed. As he and the officers went to leave his mother, woken by the noise, approached them and asked 'what the trouble was.' Bastable replied that they were police officers and that Peter was coming with them to assist with some enquiries into his movements. The officers went with Peter to Croydon Police Station. He was not under arrest so was not handcuffed, and was not cautioned before making his statement. Peter was apparently put in a 'detention room' initially but not in a cell, and was clearly still at liberty. Inspector Bastable got him a cup of tea, and he was later allowed to have a nap, undisturbed. Later on he woke, and was led into Bastable's office, where he was interviewed. Inspector Tasker was present, and took down the statement.

In his initial account, Peter mentioned how he had met Lennie when they were at school. They had become friends, and lived near each other in Camberwell. However in 1940, during the Blitz, Lennie's house had been damaged in an air raid and he had moved with his family to Thornton Heath. Peter himself had been taken to Littlehampton under the scheme by which city children were often evacuated – away from their families – to places less at risk from air raids. After two years, Peter had returned home. Lennie, who was still at Thornton Heath, visited him. Peter learned that Lennie worked at the Red Arrow Garage in that area.[7]   Peter mentioned that he had never visited the garage itself, but he had sometimes waited near it for Lennie at the end of the latter's shift. Lennie had gone on to have other jobs, and later joined the army. At the time of the murder he was with the Pioneer Corps, stationed at Blackheath.

Peter himself had a number of different jobs. Until 25 June 1945 he had been working as a building labourer at a firm in Camberwell. By his account he left the job because he did not like it. However he had left his previous job without being formally released from it, so he did not have his national insurance cards which he would need

---

[7] Children then finished school at fourteen, so it was then normal for youths in their mid-teens to be working full time. They were not subject to compulsory military service till they were eighteen.

to find another job, the builders having let him work without them. There is some suggestion that he might have left, or been discharged, from one or both of these jobs because of his disability of which we shall learn more later.[8] Peter had not told his mother that he was out of work, and left home as usual every morning. Lennie was on leave and he and Peter met up often, visiting each other's houses, and sometimes going to the cinema.

Peter stated that on 28 June 1945, the day of the murder, he had gone out he had gone out in the morning as if to work, going to Lennie's house at Roslyn Avenue in Camberwell, by 9.30. They had spent much of the morning and early afternoon together, walking around till it was time for Lennie to go home for dinner, Peter going with him. They left Lennie's at around 2 pm, and walked to Camberwell Green. Lennie had left at about 2.45 and Peter then went to the Odeon Cinema, where he watched two films.

---

8 Frank Newsam, Home Office Memo October 1945, - Jarmain PCOM papers.

He had left the cinema at around 6.30 and had gone straight home. Lennie had visited him about half an hour later and had stayed with him for an hour or two. They then went out together, met 'a few of the lads' and spent the evening in and out of Lennie's house. Later they had gone with a soldier called Harry Armstrong, to a public house – notably not the same pub that Donald had mentioned.

Peter mentioned meeting Donald – who he referred to as Caston rather than Raycaston – in the Wickwood pub the following day, but only mentioned that the latter had asked him for cigarettes which he, Peter, had not got. That same day, Peter had earlier gone with Lennie to Camberwell Green where Lennie had gone to rejoin his regiment.

Bastable was later to state that Peter 'gave the impression of being a self-possessed young man and quite innocent.' He went on, 'it began to look as if [Donald] had told lies and that Peter had had nothing to do with the crime.' Suspicion, then, was falling towards Donald.

Suddenly there was an unexpected development. As the police officers were finalising his statement for signing, Peter jumped up from his chair and said 'Take no notice of that, I want to tell you the truth.' Suspecting that a confession to involvement in the shooting was about to follow, Inspector Bastable duly cautioned Peter in the form of words used then, 'You do not have to say anything unless you wish to do so, but what you say may be given in evidence.' Peter signed to acknowledge the caution, said 'Yes, I did it,' and then went on to give the account below.

Almost a week before the shooting, Peter had been in yet another pub in Camberwell Green. He was talking to a Canadian soldier. The soldier showed Peter a gun – here Peter confirmed that this was the weapon now in the possession of the police. The soldier mentioned that he had got the gun in the Netherlands, perhaps as a war trophy. Peter asked the soldier if he wanted to sell it. The soldier must have indicated yes, as Peter's next question was how much he wanted for it. The soldier said £5. Peter said that he'd try to get the money and meet him in the pub the following night. They did meet as planned, but when Peter said that he would get the soldier £5, the latter asked for £7 and later £8. Peter agreed the sale for £8, and agreed to give it to the soldier the following night. Peter got the money from Lennie Dunn's mother by saying that he could get a ring for her (This may have been a misunderstanding by the police officer taking the statement of what Peter actually said, as we shall see later). The third night the two men met in the pub for the last time, Peter handing over the money and receiving the firearm, with seven rounds of ammunition in it. According to Peter, he got the gun because he had 'a silly idea in my mind to hold somebody up to get some money.' Specifically he said 'I got the idea of holding up the man at the garage where Lennie used to work. It is Mr Booth and I had no idea there was a lady cashier there.' Peter mentioned that he had 'pumped' Lennie for information about the garage to see whether the place would be worth the risk of an armed robbery. However he stressed that he had not told Lennie that he planned to hold up the garage.

Peter stated, as before, that he had been with Lennie on the morning of the shooting. When he left home he went home and got his overcoat – contradicting a previous account of not having such an item. He got on a bus at Loughborough Junction near his house, and went to the town hall in Brixton, from where he caught a tram to Thornton Heath Pond. He walked around for some time till the road by the garage was fairly clear, as there had been lots of factory workers going home after work. Looking into the garage he saw the bald head of a man working beneath a car – presumably Ronald.

When he thought the time was right Peter walked into the garage. The office door was shut. He pulled out the gun, cocked it and opened the door. He noticed 'somebody standing there [wearing] a green lumber jacket and thought it was a man.' As he walked into the office, gun in hand, he saw that it was a woman, Ivy. She turned towards him and saw the gun. Had she not done so, Peter claimed, he would just have asked if there were any vacancies, and then presumably abandoned the robbery attempt. He noticed that she was counting out money – he noticed two piles of silver on top of some notes.

Peter said – in movie gangster slang – 'I'll have that, sister.' She replied 'Don't be silly.' Peter had the gun in his right hand and changed it over to his left and cocked it again, allowing one bullet to fall out, saying as he did so, 'This ain't no toy,' hoping to frighten her. She said 'Don't be absurd.' Peter said nothing more and stood wondering how to get out of this situation. He must have squeezed the trigger as there was then a loud bang. The gun went off and he heard Ivy moan. As she fell Peter grabbed the money, notes and coins.

Running out of the garage, Peter went towards the Pond. He crossed to the other side of London Road and jumped onto a bus going into Croydon. He later came down and walked along the London Road back in the direction of Camberwell. He turned up a side road and went to catch a 133 bus heading out towards London. As he did so his hat fell off. On the bus, he bought a ticket to

Brixton, and later changed onto a 35 bus, getting back home for about 7 pm.

He went straight to the lavatory, where he took out the gun, removed the magazine and emptied the live cartridges. The empty shell had stuck in the slot and he took it out with his penknife. He threw the empty shell away, but stated that he could not remember where. He hid the gun, first in a chicken-house at the back and then up the chimney. Before putting the gun up the chimney he removed the magazine, placing the live rounds back in it, but leaving the magazine out of the gun. He met Donald on Friday evening, and asked him if he had read about the shooting in the papers. When Donald had said yes, Peter had admitted to the crime. Donald, Peter stated, had said 'I knew you'd do something bleeding daft.' Peter said that he had been in desperate need of money, and Donald said 'I'll lend you some.' He gave an account of how he had showed Donald the firearm two days later, although his version differed slightly from Donald's – Peter did not mention Donald taking the gun out of the house. He also stated that he had given Donald the bullets from the gun. Peter claimed that he had told Lennie about the shooting on the very night of the crime, but that Lennie had said 'You fool.'

He then remembered that he had buried the empty cartridge case in Lennie's back garden, driving it down with a broom handle. He signed the statement, witnessed by Inspector Tasker with Bastable still present. After making the statement he had identified the gun recovered by Donald as the firearm used in the shooting, with the words, 'That's the gun I did it with. It's mine.'

At some stage on the same day, Donald returned to the house at Luxor Street, and recovered the cartridges from where they were hidden – beneath the floor under the table. He handed them to the police at Camberwell Police Station, and made a second statement which, other than referring to the bullets and Peter's being taken for questioning, was in the same terms as the previous one. Donald may never have known how close he came to being under suspicion of the murder.

Bastable and Tasker took Peter along the London Road to find the hat where it had been dropped. They had no luck at this stage. Peter was returned to the station. Bastable and Tasker went in search of Lennie. They went to Roslyn Avenue but found that he was now admitted at Kings College Hospital with stomach trouble. Lennie gave a lengthy statement about his and Peter's movements on the day of the murder, he had been with Peter for much of the day but not the crucial part. On the following day he mentioned meeting with Peter and a man called Johnny at the Wickwood pub, where they saw Donald. According to Lennie, at one stage when Peter went to the lavatory, Lennie mentioned that he (Lennie) had worked at the Red Arrow garage where the murder had taken place, and Johnny said that Peter had something to do with the shooting. However, Lennie never raised the topic with Peter, and the latter never spoke to him about it. He confirmed the account about his mother having given Peter £8 in connection with a ring. Bastable thought it clear that Lennie was not telling all he knew. However the doctor treating him advised that the police should not interrogate him further.

At 10 pm that night, at Croydon Police Station, Peter was formally charged with Ivy's murder. On being told that he would be charged, he said 'Yes, sir, that's right. I have already told you all about it. I can't say any more.' He was then charged, and said 'I have nothing further to say.'

The following day, July 4th, Peter was taken to the Croydon Magistrates Court. Inspector Bastable gave evidence and tendered Peter's statement. Peter was asked by the magistrates whether he had anything to say, he said that he did not. Peter was then formally remanded to Brixton Prison until 18th July. The Croydon *Guardian and Express* reported the proceedings, with the headline '**EIGHTEEN-YEAR-OLD BOY ON MURDER CHARGE: Woman Accountant Shot In Thornton Heath Garage**'. It referred to Ivy's husband being a private in the RAMC, and that she had served as an ambulance driver during the Blitz. No reference was made to Ivy being separated from her husband or in a relationship with her employer.

The courtroom was described as full. The London evening newspaper, the *Star*, reported the proceedings in less detail under the headline 'Garage Murder Charge : YOUTH, 18 IN COURT,' with a photograph of Peter.

Peter Jarmain, in the *Star* article (Star)

Almost immediately after the court hearing, an inquest opened at Mayday Road, Croydon (presumably at the hospital mortuary), into Ivy's death. Bastable had informed Peter that he had the right to attend, but he declined. Edward Phillips attended and identified his wife's body. Dr Walsh and Dr Haler both gave evidence.

On the same day police attended at Lennie's house at Roslyn Avenue, where a detective constable dug up the cartridge case buried at the back garden. There is no reference to a search warrant having been obtained, so this must have happened with the consent or at least the acquiescence of Lennie's parents. The following day Inspector Bastable visited Lennie Dunn's mother, Mrs Jane Harriet Dunn. She gave a statement in which she said that on 25 or 26 June, Lennie asked if she could lend Peter some money. She then asked Peter what the money was for. He said he had not been to work and he had to find money to give his own mother, and he also owed money for other things. She asked him how much he wanted. He first said seven pounds, and afterwards eight. Mrs Dunn had seven pounds put aside to buy a ring [this apparently being the account which the police probably wrote down in error when taking the statements from Peter and Lennie], she gave Peter this plus another pound, making £8 in all.

On the day after the shooting, Jane was at home with her husband, Peter and

Lennie. Her husband was reading the newspaper story about the robbery. Jane said 'Red Arrow Garage, why, Lennie used to work there. What a terrible thing – boy of 24 shooting a woman.' Peter replied 'Yes it is. I don't suppose they meant to kill them.'

Jane told Bastable that she did not know of anything being buried in the garden. The inspector told her that he did not believe her son's account. She replied that she would visit Lennie in hospital and advise him to tell all that he knew.

Mrs Dunn apparently visited her son as promised. When the police attended at the hospital later, Lennie was more forthcoming. In his subsequent statement he said that he had not told the police previously that Peter had admitted involvement in the shooting, because he did not want to betray his friend (in his words 'shop his mate').

He stated that on 28 June he had gone to the cinema at the Regal Cinema, Camberwell, at around 3.10 pm and left at around half past six in the evening. After going home for his tea, he went to Peter's and arrived there about 7pm. Peter was there, and they both went out to meet some friends at Flaxman Road. Lennie identified the two friends they met as 'Sammy' and 'Johnny' but indicated that he did not know them that well to give full addresses of either – maybe he was reluctant to 'shop' them in any way. Peter had apparently told all three of them that he had gone to the garage at Thornton Road expecting to find a man but instead found a woman. Lennie then related Peter's account of the robbery, including his remark about the gun not being a toy, the accidental discharge of the firearm, his taking of the money and his escape. He had not said whether Ivy was injured or not, only that she had screamed when the gun went off.

On Saturday 30 June, Lennie met Peter again. This time he 'looked very worried and said that the woman had died.' He also said 'I didn't think she would die.' Lennie claimed that he had not known that Peter had a gun until after the latter had confessed to the shooting. He, Lennie had never seen the firearm, and Peter only told him after the shooting that he had bought the gun from a soldier. In addition Lennie said he did not know of anything being buried in their garden, nor could he remember Peter asking him anything about the Red Arrow Garage recently. Peter had also told him that after the shooting he had dumped his hat but did not say where.

The police, despite Peter's full confession, were determined to follow up any leads. They carried house to house searches in the area where Peter reported discarding his hat. On 5 July officers took a statement from a Mrs Irene Quickenden of Linden Avenue, Thornton Heath. She reported having seen a brown trilby hat on the ground 'screwed up and partly inside-out', while she had been walking along a path between Nutfield Road and Severstone Road (part of Peter's escape route). It had not been dirty and seemed to be in a good condition. She had not picked it up or examined it. She recalled the hat as being brown in colour. The following day a Mr Sidney Rogers found such a hat at Melfort Road, not far away. He handed it to the police, who in turn showed it to Mrs Quickenden. In a further statement of 9 July she confirmed that it looked like the one she had seen. Bastable later wrote that the hat was later shown to Peter's mother. She had not confirmed that it was his, but said that it might be.

5 July was also an important day in the country at large. The wartime coalition led by Winston Churchill had ended and a general election was held. The results would take some time to calculate, as service personnel posted overseas had the right to vote and their ballots had to be received and counted. Peter, Lennie and Donald – and others of their age group – would not have been entitled to vote, as the relevant age was then twenty-one.

Chapter Three: Awaiting Trial

Peter was now on remand in Brixton Prison. He had every knowledge of the possible fate that awaited him if convicted. He had been eighteen and a half years old at the time of the shooting. The law then provided that any person found guilty of murder and who was eighteen or older at the time of the crime, would be sentenced to death by hanging. The judge would have no discretion.[9] It would them be up to the Home Secretary to decide whether the sentence would be carried out or whether it would be changed to life imprisonment.

Peter was born on 4 January 1927. His father, Alfred Alexander Jarmain, was born in 1877 and was thus fifty when Peter was born. Alfred had been married in 1900 to Mary Ann Spreadsbury, who died in childbirth in 1903, the child dying not long after. As far as can be gleaned, Alfred had then lived with a woman called Jane Jones, who

---

[9] There was one exception but it could not apply to Peter! If a woman was pregnant at the time of her conviction, she would be sentenced to life imprisonment rather than to death.

he seems never to have married even though they lived together as man and wife. Family history relates that Jane was in fact the midwife who had attended Mary at her ill-fated pregnancy. They had seven children - sadly only three survived into adulthood - and in 1917 Jane herself died. In 1921, Alfred married twenty-six-year-old Emily Vincent. They had four children, Betty (born 1921), Sydney (born 1924), Peter, a sister born in 1929 who does not feature in this narrative, and the youngest brother R____, born in 1932.

At the age of seven, Peter fell and developed a serious leg injury. According to a family source, it had happened at a time when a lodger's child caught chickenpox or measles. Back then it was apparently customary that if one child in a house caught such a disease, to keep the rest of the children in until they all had it, and thus 'get it out of the way.' However little Peter had wanted to play outside in the street. As he was going out of the door, his eldest sister caught him. He ran back into the front room, and tripped, falling on some wood that had been brought in to light the fire.

One of the pieces had a rusty nail sticking out and it went through Peter's knee. He went on to spend two years in hospital, having several operations at King's College Hospital.[10] He developed septicaemia, and had to wear a calliper on the affected leg. He later told of the name-calling and bullying he suffered from other children as a result. The leg injury also seems to have led to Peter having what was later described by a doctor as 'a rheumatic heart.'

Peter went on to be admitted at the Queen Mary Hospital for Sick Children at Carshalton for some two years. His mother made the long journey from Camberwell every day to visit him. On his discharge, he attended the Venetia Road School, described as a 'school for cripples' – it is said that he was taken to the school in an ambulance every day.[11] Peter would later state that the disability and linked illness caused him to have an inferiority complex. Reportedly he walked with a limp afterwards, although perhaps not so noticeable as it

---

[10] *Croydon Advertiser* 28 Sept 1945

[11] *Croydon Advertiser* 28 Sept 1945

seems not to be mentioned in any of the witness statements. There is no record that he was ever called up into the armed forces, so his disability may have had an effect in that regard.

In 1941 Peter turned 14, the age at which children then left school and could enter the workforce. even though they would not be legally adult for another seven years. Sadly that year also brought tragedy – Alfred Jarmain passed away at the age of 64, of meningitis and other complications. He had worked as a basket-maker and presumably had brought in a decent income, which was now gone. His widow Emily reportedly made ends meet in part by 'wet-nursing,' breast-feeding the children of rich families.

Peter was soon the oldest of the children still at home, as his elder siblings joined the forces – Betty late in 1941, Sidney in mid-1943. He flung himself into the world of work , and held a number of jobs in succession. By all accounts, he tried hard to bring in money and help support his mother. Reportedly, despite working during the day, he also volunteered for 'fire-watching' duty for three years. This involved taking up position on rooftops and extinguishing falling incendiary bombs with sand or water.

He worked at a solicitors' firm in Holborn for about six weeks as a telephone boy. After that, he worked at a local boot repair shop for some six months. There followed a sixteen-month stint as a labourer at a timber yard in the local area. He went on to work for three weeks at an aircraft factory in Brixton, before going to be a van boy at a brewer's in Camberwell. It must have been this job which he left without being formally released and thus not having his national insurance cards. A builders' firm in Vauxhall took him on and he stayed with them for six weeks, it was his departure from that firm which left him short of money and hiding his unemployment from his mother.

He was described as slim, with a slight moustache, and smartly dressed. He would wear a check jacket of the sort known as 'Prince of Wales', [after the former Prince, by then the Duke of Windsor, who wore such jackets] and often sported a trilby hat. His friends gave him the nickname 'Trinder', after the popular comedian and film star Tommy Trinder, another trilby-wearing smart dresser.

A number of letters from Peter, or about him, give some clue to his mindset while in prison. As to the letters from him, Peter may not have been aware that any letters sent to or from him were monitored by the prison authorities. Any sent by him were copied and the copy sent to the Home Office. Such letters, if incriminating, could form part of the case against a prisoner. Likewise, if a prisoner was convicted of murder and sentenced to death, such letters could assist the Home Secretary in deciding whether their life should be spared.

An undated letter presumably sent on around 4 July 1945 was addressed to a Miss Doris Young of Hilda Road, Brixton. Reading between the lines she seems to have been an ex-girlfriend. The letter reads:

"Dear Doris,

Just a little line hoping this finds you O.K. I suppose by the time you get this letter you'll know how I am.

Would you go round to see how my Mum is you might be able to comfort her a little. I find you are the only one I can ask please will you do this for old time's sake. I've got a very little chance of not hanging the facts are so much against me.

How's things going with you? [....]Write and lets know a letter's a great comfort, maybe asking too much but think it over. I've no hard feelings against you. Please write and ask George to if you can see him. Thanks.

Will close now as I can't find anything else to say, look after yourself.

From

Pete."

The above letter is quite grim in Peter's assessment of his prospects. Days later he wrote to some other friends (including 'Sam,' and 'Johnny', some of the people Lennie mentioned in his statement).

This time while he acknowledges the grave position he is in, he is in parts optimistic, applying black humour (unfortunately also called 'gallows humour') to his situation. It seems that Doris had visited him in the meantime, possibly accompanied by his eldest sister.

"Brixton Prison

Dear Sam and Boys

Just a line to say that I [am] OK and enjoying a qui[et] rest at the address above. (some hope)

Doris came with Betty yesterday to see me, she's a good kid, pity I didn't stick to her when I had the chance, I wouldn't have been in the fix I'm in now, but some day, I hope, a very long time from now, I'll be out and I'll make it up to you all and pay the debt I ow[e] to some-one, I don't know who yet but will find out when he gives evidence against me.

Send me a little letter now and again it gives you something to think about and helps to pass the time away. I'm [on] remand here till the 26th July and they will size it up and I suppose I will be remanded again until sometime in September as no assizes run in August, so you see I live, if not for long, for a little while.[12]

How's Johnny going with the boys, and how's your dad Sam. I know how Johnny's old man is.

Well I can't find any more to say except look after my old lady for me and write soon.

Cheerio for now

From your old Pal
(3679) Pete (Trinder)"

There is a contrast between the earlier part of the letter, where Peter mentions his hope for release at some time in the fu-

---

[12] The Assizes were the equivalent of the present day Crown Court, trying serious criminal cases including murder, robbery and rape.

ture, and the latter part. Towards the end he acknowledges the possibility of an early death, but in jest. This tendency towards black humour may have soon caused a person of some importance to form an unfavourable impression of Peter, as we shall see.

As he had predicted, Peter soon learnt who the main witness against him was. He returned to the magistrate's court on 26 July. Reginald Booth gave evidence as to the shooting and aftermath. Witnesses gave evidence of Ivy's death – Dr Haler, Ivy's brother, and a nursing sister from the Mayday. Crucially, Donald gave evidence, as did Lennie's mother. All of them testified in line with their statements. Inspector Bastable was recalled, giving more detailed evidence than beforehand. The court formally committed Peter to stand trial at the Central Criminal Court (London's famous 'Old Bailey'), for 22 September 1945.

On the same day as the court hearing, the results of the general election were announced. The opposition Labour party won their first ever absolute majority. Winston

Churchill, Britain's prime minister for much of the war, was defeated and went into opposition.

The case against Peter seemed watertight, but Inspector Bastable still had work to do. He had been in the Metropolitan Police for thirty years. Policing was in his blood. His father had been a policeman as well, attaining the rank of Superintendent and being awarded the MBE on retirement after forty years' service. Bastable was on the verge of retirement himself. The detective may have felt some sympathy for Peter's mother, as he himself had a son not much older than Peter.

In August, as the trial approached, he wrote letters, with scrupulous even-handedness, to various military authorities concerning the upcoming hearing. He wrote to Edward Phillips's commanding officer, and Sydney Jarmain's, asking for them to be given leave to attend the trial. He also wrote to Betty Jarmain's superiors, asking for her to be given a compassionate discharge to be able to look after her mother, as Peter was unlikely to return home anytime soon come what may. Edward's superiors refused the request. Sydney was granted the requested leave. Betty was not given a full discharge, but a temporary one.

Bastable's sympathy for Emily shows in some of his letters. In his letter dated 2 August 1945, to Betty's WAAF superiors, he writes:

"Mrs Jarmain is a hardworking woman and in view of the amount of worry and trouble that her son is causing her, I am of the opinion that this is a case where sympathetic consideration might be given to [Betty's] application."

In an earlier report to his superintendent, he stated:

"[Peter's] home, although poor, is clean and his mother is a hard working woman."

Bastable also had trouble with his star witness. Donald had stated that he had not served in the military due to being a tuberculosis sufferer, and Bastable had felt that his appearance supported this. However, the young man seemed evasive. When attending the magistrates' court, he was unable to produce his identity card, stating that he had misplaced it and that he was seeking another one, his existing card already being a replacement. Bastable had suspected that something was amiss, and had Tasker check the register of deserters and the criminal records office. There was no trace of a 'Donald Raycaston' in either.

On 20th August 1945, the police made enquiries were made at Donald's address in Camberwell, to serve him with a 'recognisance' (a bond to secure his attendance at the trial). The police found out that Donald had moved without leaving a forwarding address, owing rent. Further enquiries at his employer showed that he had left earlier in the month. He had worked briefly at another transport firm, and had left there on 17 August, having received his insurance cards.

Bastable and Tasker made investigations in Camberwell, Peckham and Brixton, to trace Donald. They noted that the name 'Raycaston' was unusual and there was no trace of anyone with that name. They then started to look for similar names. The following name came up: D. R Caston, of the Anti-Aircraft Corps, who had deserted since 14 January 1945. Further enquiries revealed that the man's full name was Donald Ray Caston. It can be recalled that in his statement Peter always referred to Donald as 'Caston.' Maybe Peter knew his real identity and that he was a deserter.

Donald Caston's home address was at Earlham in Norwich – he had been born in that county some twenty years earlier. The London police contacted their counterparts in Norwich, who then checked on Donald's mother. She was unable to give any information about where Donald was.

However the continuing enquiries came to Donald's ears. He duly attended at Brixton Police Station. Initially he denied being Caston the deserter, but a message was sent to Norwich police who confirmed with Donald's mother certain tattoos that Caston had. She also stated that her son's second name was 'Ray.' The game was up. Maybe Donald's motivation for reporting Peter's crimes was a fear of being caught as a deserter and implicated in a murder. While deserters were no longer shot for that crime as they had been in the previous war, such a person accused of involvement in murder could expect little mercy.

Donald was charged with being a deserter, appearing at Lambeth Magistrates Court on 5 September. He was initially given bail in the sum of £50, with two sureties in equal sums. This was not forthcoming, and Donald was remanded into custody for 10 September. His unit was contacted, and the Army Special Investigation Branch (the military police's equivalent of a civilian police CID) agreed to detain Caston until after Peter's trial. Donald agreed to give evidence as in his statement.

It seems that Peter's first few days in prison were spent in a hospital setting, although presumably he was able to receive visitors as we have seen. One might wonder why a young man in reasonably good health would spend time in hospital just after his arrival, as they would normally only need the briefest of medical checkups.

The answer lies in the offence Peter was charged with, and the maximum penalty for it. While many murderers were executed in those days, the state also sought to ensure that those who were mentally ill to the point of being insane, did not suffer such a fate. Doctors examined murder suspects for mental as well as physical health. Anyone found to be insane would not be found fit for trial, and would be sent to a secure mental hospital indefinitely. Likewise a person charged with murder could be found 'guilty but insane' by the trial jury [the present-day verdict would be 'not guilty by reason of insanity'], and be sent to such a hospital likewise.

Even people already convicted of murder could be found insane afterwards, and then they would be sent to such a hospital, or to prison, rather than hanged. Such a reprieve might be a mixed blessing, as they would usually spend far longer in detention than other murderers spared from the gallows. An extreme example is that of John Straffen, who killed three young girls in the early 1950s. He was convicted of murder in 1952, reprieved, and spent the rest of his long life in prison, dying there in 2007, aged 77.[13]

The insanity ground was widely deployed at various stages of the criminal process. For example, in 1952, out of sixty-five people charged with murder in England and Wales , fifteen were found unfit to plead, and seventeen found guilty but insane. Even out of the thirty-three found guilty of murder and duly sentenced to death, one was found insane post-conviction and sent to be detained at a secure mental hospital. Thus just over half were found insane in one way or another.[14]

Peter may not have known the purpose of this hospital stay. Dr Hugh Grierson, the prison medical officer who examined him, wrote a detailed report for the Director of Public Prosecutions. In the report, dated 31 August 1945, the doctor states that Peter had been under observation in the hospital since 4 July 1945, thus since the day he was remanded in custody. The

[13] *Somerset News* 21 March 2018

[14] FA Newsam, *The Home Office*, George Allen and Unwin, 1954, p. 116

doctor notes that he had interviewed Peter, his sister Betty, and some prison officers who had been in contact with Peter. He went through Peter's medical history as stated above.

Dr Grierson commented that Peter, 'conversed and conducted himself normally, 'and at no time has he exhibited signs of insanity.' The report continues, 'Discussion of the charge elicits a considerable degree of callousness with a poor moral outlook.' Sadly the doctor did not note what response of Peter's led to this observation. Perhaps Peter felt at ease in the doctor's company and fell into his dark humour, which the doctor would have seen as insensitive. Alternatively it may be that Peter narrated the events of the shooting in a very matter-of-fact way, which might have been seen as callous.

The doctor concluded that he had not found any evidence of mental disease 'which would prevent him from knowing what he was doing and that what he was doing was wrong,' [this was, and is, the legal test for insanity under the 'Macnaghten

Rules'], and stated that Peter was fit to plead.

In the world outside, life went on. As soldiers returned home, tensions arose among those who felt their way back was being obstructed. On the very day of Peter's first appearance at the magistrates court, Canadian troops were on the second day of a riot in the garrison town of Aldershot, frustrated at delays in their repatriation – they felt that American soldiers were getting priority over them in the allocation of space on the troopships. At the same time, British and other allied forces in Burma were engaged in the bloody Battle of Sittang Bend, as the war in the Far East ground on.

Elsewhere in London another young man slightly younger than Peter, was also preparing to go on trial for his life. His case arose from a rather unlikely series of events which had taken place during the recent conflict in Europe. In late 1944 and early 1945, as Allied forces secured their position in mainland Europe and advanced against the Germans, the number of enemy prisoners held in camps in Britain itself increased greatly. It would have been clear to most of them that the tide had turned and that Germany would lose the war. However the camps were also home to a number of fanatical Nazis who refused to believe the war was lost. They constantly planned to escape and return home to fight again. Some may even have believed that they could arm themselves, free other prisoners, and march on London, helping to turn the tide of the war.[15] One of the planned escapes coincided with a major German attack on Allied forces in Belgium, the Ardennes Offensive. The prisoners hoped that their escape and subsequent operations would assist in the counter-attack on the Continent.

In two cases failed escape attempts lead to tragedy. The first was at a prison camp near Comrie in Perthshire, Scotland. An escape attempt by Nazis had recently been foiled at a camp in Wiltshire, and the men affected were moved to the high-security camp in Scotland. The would-be es-

---

[15] *The March on London* by Charles Whiting, Pen and Sword, 1992.

capees believed that one of their fellow prisoners had betrayed their plans to the British guards. On the night of 23 December 1944, the suspected informant, Wolfgang Rosterg was woken by his Nazi fellow-prisoners and a rope put around his neck. After a mock trial, he was severely beaten and dragged to the lavatories, where he was hanged from a pipe. He was probably dead from the beating by then anyway, but the prisoners hoped that his death would appear to be a suicide[16]. The guards were not so convinced, and eight of the Nazi prisoners were detained for the murder.

A similar story unfolded at another camp, Lodge Moor near Sheffield in Yorkshire, early the following year. Again, this was a camp containing large numbers of Nazis who planned to escape. An escape tunnel was found by the guards, and one of the prisoners was suspected of treachery. This suspect was a 25 year old sergeant named Gerhart Rettig. He was known by the other prisoners to be a non-Nazi, and felt he was at risk. Fatefully, he spoke to the

---

[16] See the similar scene in the 1970 prisoner-of-war drama film *The McKenzie Break*.

British guards about a possible transfer to another camp. He was seen by other prisoners and his fate was sealed.[17] On the morning of 24 March 1945 as Rettig was seen packing his kit-bag prior to being moved, he and another 'suspect', Huth, were attacked by a mob of prisoners. Huth seems to have escaped serious injury, but Rettig was severely beaten. British soldiers were able to rescue Rettig at length, but he died in hospital not long afterwards. Huth was able to identify some of the attackers, and four prisoners suspected of involvement were detained.

The detainees seem to have been kept under 'open arrest' rather than in close confinement. In fact, two of them escaped from the camp a few days later- by simply crawling under the wire - only to be swiftly recaptured.[18] One of the detainees - not one of the ones who briefly escaped - was a young airman called Armin Kühne.

[17] Apparently the plan *had* been betrayed, but not by Rettig: *Churchill's Unexpected Guests: Prisoners of War in Britain in World War II* by Sophie Jackson, The History Press 2010.

[18] *Yorkshire Post* and *Leeds Mercury* 10 August 1945.

Armin was about three weeks younger than Peter, having been born on 28 January 1927 at Gera in the eastern German state of Thuringia. He was one of a large family. At the time, Germany was in a state of flux following defeat in the First World War. The German Empire, ruled by the *Kaiser* (Emperor) had been overthrown and replaced by the Weimar Republic. The latter regime was saddled with huge debts for wartime reparations.   Between 1918 and 1924 the country was affected by severe inflation, with prices rising and the currency losing value.   Afterwards, the 1929 worldwide economic downturn hit Germany harder than it did many other leading economies.

In this climate, people flocked to the extremes of left and right, supporting the Communists and the new far-right Nazi Party. Thuringia had Germany's first ever Nazi Party minister as early as 1930, albeit as part of a coalition in the state government. Three years later, when Armin was only six, the Nazis came to power in Berlin. The party's leader Adolf Hitler became head of government, later also becoming head of state on President Hindenburg' s death.

Hitler's party sought to entrench its power by instructing young people in Nazi thinking. Youth organisations such as the Hitler Youth were set up to do this.

In the early 1930s the Kühnes left Gera and moved to Schwerin, in the northern province of Mecklenburg. Shortly before this the family had gone through some turmoil. While Armin's mother Helene had been pregnant, his father Herbert had a relationship with their female housekeeper. This resulted in the housekeeper becoming pregnant, and both women gave birth to daughters within months of each other. The housekeeper's daughter was brought up by Herbert's sister.[19]

Armin reportedly joined the Hitler Youth aged nine, and left home at twelve, having become a Hitler Youth group leader. Afterwards he went to specialised schools. By the age of fifteen, he was engaged in instruction of other youths in '[Nazi] philoso-

---

[19] Personal communication from Marco Mjundhenk, Oct 2018.

phy with particular emphasis on the life of [Hitler].'[20]

By now war had broken out. The family, or some members of it, seems to have spent some time in Sieradz, a part of occupied Poland chosen to be 'Germanised', i.e settled by ethnic Germans with the original population expelled. Armin's little sister Hedwig died there in 1941, aged four. Males of all ages were called up, or volunteered – there are pictures of Herbert Kühne, aged about forty, in army uniform. Armin's brother Manfred also joined up – later to be killed in action in Poland in 1944, aged eighteen.

Armin Kühne (Marco Mundhenk)

The exact date of Armin's own enlistment is not available. However, it seems that he joined the forces under-age, possibly - like many youths before and since – by giving a wrong date of birth. He joined the *Luftwaffe* (air force) although he seems not to have been aircrew trained. He apparently served as a combat medic, and later claimed to have served at a front-line dressing station. A note from him to his family, scribbled on the back of the photo shown here, indicates that in late June 1944 he was 'on the battlefield', presumably somewhere in Western Europe. Allied forces captured him in October of that year when he was a few months short of eighteen. By then he was a *San-Gefreiter*, (acting lance corporal). He remained a fanatical Nazi in the prisoner of war camps, hence his involvement in the murderous attack on the alleged informer Rettig. He was later described as being five feet five inches tall – that is about 165 centimetres - and slightly built.

The men involved in the two prisoner-of-war killings could not be tried until the war in Europe ended, as this might have caused reprisals against family members back home of any German prisoners giving evidence against their fellows. Their trials were scheduled to take place in July and August. The murder of Rosterg had happened in Scotland, where the law of murder was different from that in England. Conviction in a civilian court there would then have required a number of witnesses that the prosecution could not be sure of. So that matter, and later that of Rettig's murder, were tried by the military, which operated under English law with its simpler rules of evidence.

In London, meanwhile, preparations were underway for Peter's trial. His solicitors would have come up against a difficult point of law in the case, the 'felony murder' rule. Then as now, if a person struck another intending to kill them, or intending to seriously injure them, and that other person died, the first person would be guilty of murder. However, in 1945 there was another category of murder. If someone struck another while committing a violent 'felony' – that is, a violent 'serious offence,' then if the second person died as a result the first person would be guilty of murder, even if the attacker had not intended to kill or cause serious injury.

Over the centuries, the courts in England and Wales had restricted this rule, in practice, to cases of robbery and rape. Thus in October 1919 a man named Arthur Beard was convicted of murder, having covered the mouth of the girl he was raping, and inadvertently causing her death. He was convicted of murder and sentenced to hang. However the Court of Criminal Appeal overturned the murder conviction, and convicted him of manslaughter, largely on the basis of his alleged drunkenness at the time of the offence. His death sentence was replaced by one of imprisonment. However the prosecution then appealed to the highest court at the time, the House of Lords. Early the following year they reinstated the original conviction and sentence of death. Fortunately for Beard, he was reprieved.

Any idea that the passage of two decades might lead to a change of approach from the judges had gone earlier in the year. We have already seen how the American soldier, Karl Hulten, and his accomplice Betty Jones were convicted earlier of murder during a robbery. This was despite Hulten's claim that he had not deliberately fired his gun at the taxi driver victim. Ominously, the Crown chose the barrister who had prosecuted that matter, Laurence Byrne, to present the case against Peter. A barrister of some thirty years standing, he had been a senior government prosecutor for many years. He had recently declined the top prosecution job, that of Director of Public Prosecutions. He had been a 'Recorder,' a part-time judge, for six years.

The trial solicitors would presumably have told Peter about this legal position. Perhaps this was what he meant when he wrote to Doris stating that he had little chance of not being hanged as the facts were so much against him. The solicitors seem to have been appointed by the legal aid organisation, and the name of the firm does not appear in any documents that the author has so far seen. They instructed barrister Frederick Lawton to defend Peter at his trial.

Aged thirty-four, Lawton had been called to the Bar ten years previously. He came from rather humble circumstances compared to many of his fellow barristers. He had been born at Wandsworth in London, where his father William was a prison governor (the first ever to rise from the ranks). Lawton had spent most of his childhood in officer quarters within prisons. Later in his career at the Bar he would retort to a habitual criminal, when the latter complained about prison conditions, 'I don't believe you. I have spent more time in prison than you.'[21]   He went on to attend Battersea Grammar School, and then went to university at Cambridge.

In Britain as in Germany, the turbulent inter-war years drew many to the political extremes. Lawton was reported to have 'flirted with Communism'[22] while at university, but after his studies he went to the opposite political side and joined the far-right British Union of Fascists. That party had selected him as a parliamentary can-

---

[21] *Daily Telegraph*, 6 February 2001

[22] *Telegraph*, ibid

didate for Hammersmith. Fortunately no election was called at the time, and Lawton seems to have left the party around the outbreak of war in 1939.

He then spent two years in the Army before being discharged through injury. In 1942 he had defended his first murder, the Blitz case of Harry Dobkin, mentioned earlier. Lawton's advocacy - in the Old Bailey and the Court of Criminal Appeal - had not been enough to save Dobkin's life, but he was generally held to have conducted the case well. One author wrote 'In a most difficult case, against overwhelming odds and with heavy medical evidence against him, Mr Lawton did everything - except the impossible.'[23]

Early in August, US aircraft dropped atom bombs on the Japanese cities of Hiroshima and Nagasaki, causing tens of thousands of deaths. Japan surrendered unconditionally on August 14, bringing the war to an end. Celebrations erupted across the Allied countries. In Britain a two-day public

---

[23] *The Trial of Harry Dobkin*, 'Old Bailey Trial Series', by C E Bechhofer Roberts, (Jarrolds, 1944)

holiday was declared, starting with 'V-J' (Victory in Japan) Day on August 15. For tens of thousands of service personnel in the Far East and elsewhere, the possibility of an early death had receded. But for Peter and Armin it still loomed large.

Chapter Four: The Trial

Just within the former walls of the old City of London – the mile-square area in the centre of the wider region which we now know as London – lies the courthouse called the Old Bailey. Its impressive, domed appearance calls to mind an old cathedral – London's St Paul's maybe, or St Peter's in Rome. But the Old Bailey – the current building at least – is nowhere near as old. It dates back a little over a century, having been opened in 1902 – although predecessor buildings nearby bore the same nickname. Its official title is more imposing – it is formally called 'The Central Criminal Court of England and Wales.' Its reach is even further than indicated, as it can try crimes committed at sea, or murder committed by British citizens anywhere.

The area has been hallowed turf for the criminal justice system for much longer, as the current court was built on the site of the former Newgate Prison. It was from Newgate – built in the Middle Ages - that convicted prisoners had been taken to the gallows at Tyburn[24] in the seventeenth and early nineteenth century and earlier, when most 'felonies' - even the non-violent ones like theft - could carry the death penalty. Even when executions were no longer held at Tyburn, they took place in front of Newgate, where the last public hanging in Britain was carried out in 1868.

In the early years of the twentieth century, the old prison was demolished and the new courthouse put up. Atop its roof was the familiar figure of Justice, a statue of a woman carrying scales with which to judge the defendant and a sword to punish them if found guilty – this image, unlike similar ones found elsewhere, is not blindfolded. The lofty ideals behind its construction may be seen in the words carved over the entrance; 'Defend the Children of the Poor and Punish the Wrongdoer.'

In the latter part of September 1945, in Court One of the Old Bailey, a man was on trial for his life. Journalists, local and foreign, reported the proceedings daily, in

---

[24] Now Marble Arch

many languages. The story, related over newspapers, in newsreels and over the radio, gripped the attention of the world. While the man had definitely committed the acts that brought him to court, his defence turned on a fine point of law.

The man was William Joyce, better known by a nickname we shall soon learn. He had been born in New York some forty years earlier, to an Irish father who had become a naturalised American. Shortly after his birth his family had moved back to Galway in the south of Ireland, and later to England when most of Ireland gained its independence in the early 1920s. In the 1930s, like so many others, he had joined the British Union of Fascists. Unlike Frederick Lawton, he was still a supporter of Fascism when the war started. Knowing that he faced preventive detention, known as 'internment', if he were still in Britain when the conflict broke out, Joyce fled to Germany before the declaration of war. He travelled on a British passport obtained by fraudulently claiming to have been born in Ireland, all of which had been a part of the UK at the time of his birth.

In Germany, Joyce had broadcast propaganda in English for his new hosts. His trademark drawl became instantly recognisable to British listeners. Although they were discouraged from listening to German broadcasts many people did, partly to laugh at the exaggerated boasts and claims, but also to glean information about the war which the British censors might be suppressing. There were many such broadcasters, but Joyce became the most well-known - and the most hated. Music-hall comedians would bring the house down with an impression of his broadcast introduction, imitating his affected pronunciation: 'Jairmany Calling! Jairmany Calling!'[25] His mocking voice brought him the name 'Lord Haw-Haw.'

Arrested shortly after the collapse of Nazi Germany, Joyce was brought back to Britain for trial. His defence was that he was not a British subject at all, as he had been born abroad at a time when his father was a naturalised American and therefore no longer had British citizenship to pass on.

[25] *Trial of William Joyce,* C E Bechhofer Roberts, Jarrolds, 1946

Thus, he argued, he could not be guilty of treason. In the three day trial, starting on 17 September, the Crown argued otherwise. The prosecution lawyers - including Laurence Byrne - argued that even though Joyce's passport was obtained by fraud, it entitled him to protection from the British Government. As a result, they said, he had a duty of loyalty to the country. The jury accepted this argument and found Joyce guilty. He was duly sentenced to death.[26]

Just a few days later, on the morning of the 25 September Peter Jarmain walked into the same dock in Court One, for the start of his own trial. The indictment alleged:

'PETER JOSEPH JARMAIN was charged for that he on the 30th day of June, 1945, in the County Borough of Croydon, feloniously, wilfully and of his malice aforethought did kill and murder one Ivy May Phillips against the peace of our Sov-

---

[26] His appeals were dismissed, and there was no reprieve. He was executed at Wandsworth Prison on 3 January 1946

ereign Lord the King, His Crown and Majesty.'

Looking around at the public gallery Peter would have seen some familiar faces. Dr Grierson, the medical officer at Brixton, was there. Peter's mother would definitely have attended. His brother Sydney and sister Betty - having obtained special leave in Sydney's case, and a temporary discharge in Betty's – would have been there too. Peter may have noticed, but probably not recognised, another person in uniform. Edward Phillips – Ivy's husband - had unexpectedly secured leave to follow the trial.

Shortly beforehand, Peter would probably have met Frederick Lawton for the first time. This followed then-current English legal usage – the person who would have visited him in prison and discussed the case with him would be his solicitor, who would instruct a barrister. It would only be on the first day of the trial that the solicitor would introduce the defendant (then called 'the prisoner' in felony cases even if they were on bail) to the barrister.

Lawton may well have explained his plan to Peter. As we have seen, if the court held that Peter had shot Ivy while in the course of an armed robbery, this would be murder because the killing, accidental or not, happened during a 'felony.' Lawton hoped to show that at the time the gun went off Peter had given up on the robbery and was just pondering his next move with a view to escaping. The shooting would therefore be an accident when not committing a felony – this would amount to manslaughter not murder. The sentence would be a maximum of life in prison, although people usually received shorter sentences.

The barristers all sat at the second row of the area reserved for barristers. Mr Lawton appeared on his own, while Mr Boyd Carpenter appeared alongside Mr Byrne for the prosecution. The first row was empty because none of the barristers were 'King's Counsel,' the most senior rank of barristers.

The court rose as the judge entered, wearing red robes and a wig. Byrne would have been encouraged when he had learned who the judge was, Lawton quite the opposite. The judge was Sir Ernest Charles, who had presided over the trial of Karl Hulten and Betty Jones earlier in the year.

The court went through the initial formalities. The clerk to the court, seated below the judge in a black gown and wearing a wig, addressed Peter.

'Peter Joseph Jarmain, you are charged with the murder of Ivy May Phillips on the thirtieth of June next. Are you guilty or not guilty?'

Peter replied 'Not guilty.'

The jury was duly sworn, it comprised ten men and two women.

The clerk went on 'Members of the jury, the prisoner at the bar, Peter Joseph Jarmain, is charged with the murder of Ivy May Phillips on the thirtieth of June last. To this indictment he has pleaded not guilty, and it is your charge to say, having heard the evidence, whether he be guilty or not.'

Mr Byrne rose to open the case for the prosecution. 'As you have heard, the charge that is made against [Peter] is a charge of murder, he is charged with the murder of a woman named Ivy May Phillips. She was a married woman and was employed as clerk and cashier by a Mr Booth, who is the proprietor of a garage at Thornton Heath, the Red Arrow garage, Thornton Road, Thornton Heath.' He went on to outline the Crown's case against Peter, referring to the witnesses due to give evidence and what they were expected to say. He concluded:

'If you are satisfied, when you have heard the whole of the evidence in this case, that the Prisoner fired at the deceased woman, either with the intention of killing her in order to effect the robbery, or with the intention of causing her grievous bodily harm in order to effect the robbery, then that would be murder; and moreover, in the submission of the Prosecution, it would equally be murder if, upon [hearing] the whole of the evidence, you c a m e to the conclusion that in the course of committing the felony of robbery armed the Prisoner quite inadvertently caused the death of that woman by shooting her.'

The prosecution called its first witness, PC Cyril Weir. He tendered the plan of the Red Arrow Garage. Mr Lawton only asked him a few questions in cross-examination, relating to the streets in the neighbourhood and how busy the area would have been at the time of the offence.

The next witness was Lennie Dunn's mother Harriet. She gave evidence that her son was in the Army, and that he, and she, both new Peter. She also told how Peter had been short of money, and had borrowed her ring money, also allegedly stating that Peter had claimed to know someone who could supply a ring. Her evidence was quickly over, Mr Lawton choosing not to cross-examine.

Ronald Booth was then called. He gave evidence that he owned the garage, and that Ivy had been employed there. He also testified about the shooting and its immediate aftermath, and about the money missing from the till.

Mr Lawton cross-examined briefly about the garage. Mr Booth confirmed that they had been open to the public at the time, and that they would have been till midnight. He confirmed where people would have been working on the site, and that explosions were frequent in garages. He stated that if an explosion took place that did seem to be out of the ordinary, someone could be on the spot within seconds.

Next was Winifred Williams, a nursing sister at the Mayday Hospital. She gave evidence about Ivy's admission to hospital, her treatment and subsequent death. Ivy's brother Mr H____ Johns was the next witness. He gave evidence that he had identified Ivy's body.

Dr David Haler, the pathologist, was next to testify. He gave evidence about Ivy's injuries, summing up by confirming that the cause of death had been 'shock and haemorrhage from a bullet wound in the liver.'

Mr Lawton cross-examined him. In response to the barrister's question, Dr Haler confirmed that he had some interest in firearms and their working. The pistol used, Exhibit 'E', was produced. Mr Lawton took

Dr Haler through the workings of the particular pistol:

Lawton: Will you just take the pistol in your hand with the safety catch on in the correct position. In that position the pistol cannot be fired?

Haler: No.

L: Will you please release the safety catch. Assuming that the magazine was full would one be able to fire the pistol by pulling the trigger and expelling a shot at once, or would one have to do something to it?

H. No.

L: That would you have to do after releasing the safety catch in order to fire the pistol?

H: The magazine should be released. This has to be drawn back so; that places a shot in the chamber ready to fire.

L: That is what is technically known as cocking?

H: That is so.

L: And it is only then that you can fire?

H. That is so.

L: I want you to deal with the position, demonstrating it, if you can, to the jury: assuming that the pistol had been cocked with the effect of putting a round into the breech, and the man holding it wished to extract that round from the breech, what would he have to do?

H: He would have to press this knob here which releases the magazine, and then pull back that to eject it.

L: Would the effect of doing that cause the round to fall out on to the ground unless it was caught?

H: Through this hole here.

L: What would the effect be after that, what would another round be automatically put into the breech or not?

H: Not unless re-cocked?

L: It would have to be re-cocked?

H: Yes.

The next witness was Detective Sergeant William Butcher, who gave evidence about finding a cartridge at the scene of the shooting. Mr Lawton only cross-examined to elicit the answer that the cartridge found had been a live one rather than spent.

Inspector Bastable now went into the witness box. He gave evidence of how he had entered Peter's bedroom at Luxor Street, along with Inspector Tasker. He related that when woken, and informed that he was to be asked about his movements on the day of the shooting, Peter claimed that while he knew the garage, he could not help with the murder enquiry as he knew nothing about the crime. However, he had agreed to go with Bastable to give his account at the police station. He made clear that Peter, up to and including the time he was making his statement, had not been cautioned. Then, while coming to the end of his statement, he had suddenly said 'Take no notice of that. I want to tell you the truth.' Bastable had then cautioned Peter, who had then given his detailed account of the crime. The statement was read out by the clerk of the court, starting from the part where Peter was cautioned. Bastable confirmed that when the charge was formally put to him he had said 'I have nothing further to say.'

Mr Lawton then rose to cross-examine. He made it clear that he was seeking to challenge the accuracy of the statement. This was in an era where the police were generally held in far higher esteem than they are now, and accusing them outright of lying or putting words into the defendant's mouth, was a very risky strategy. Such an allegation could turn the judge, and maybe the jury, against the defendant, with fateful - maybe even fatal - consequences. In putting his question, Lawton had to phrase his words carefully.

Lawton: I am going to challenge the accuracy of that statement as taken down by Detective Inspector Tasker in only one particular, and I will identify it at once if I may. [...] you have got somewhere in that part of the statement he explained how he got on a bus at Loughborough Junction, and so on, and then he said 'I waited outside the garage until the road was pretty clear. When I thought it was the right moment I walked into the garage. The office door was shut. I pulled out the gun and cocked it and opened the door.' I am going to suggest to you, Inspector, that what happened was as a result of confusion in the room when this statement was taken those words 'cocked it and opened the door' have got in by mistake. Let us just deal with the circumstances of the matter.'

He then questioned Bastable about the detail of how Peter had been interviewed. Lawton tried to suggest that Peter had been 'suffering from some form of emotional upset' at the time of the interview, but Bastable would only agree that Peter 'was under stress.'

Lawton went into more detail:

L: Let me put it in this way: Was his method of making his statement such that the Officer taking it down could write the words as he spoke them, or was it necessary for you, being in charge of the interview, from time to time to stop him so that the Officer could go back a little and pick up the threads of the story?

Bastable: What happened was, as he said a sentence or a phrase I repeated it slowly to make sure I had got it while it was written down so there would be no...

Mr Justice Charles: 'I repeated it slowly and it was then taken down?

B: As it was being written down.

L: Did he ever correct you?

B: No, I cannot recollect that he did.

L: You see, I want to make this clear in fairness to both you and your colleague; I am not suggesting that something has got into the statement which was a sheer invention, either deliberate or inadvertent, on your part or anyone else', but what he did make clear to you in giving his story was that after he had got into the office and the woman there had told him not to be silly, it was after that he cocked the revolver twice.[27] Do you think it is possible that you have got it out of sequence?

---

[27] At the time a pistol with a repeater function was sometimes called a revolver even if it did not have a revolving drum.

B: I do not think so. I think the only time he cocked it after he got in was the once when he ejected the cartridge.

Cross-examination went on in this vein, the officer sticking to his position that there had been no scope for the officer taking down the statement having misinterpreted what Peter had said.

Lawton then changed tack and asked about character matters. In response to his questions Bastable confirmed Peter's date of birth, and that he had no previous arrests or convictions, and that his home at 10 Luxor Street was 'a respectable home.'

Another police witness gave evidence - DC Harold Hudson testified that he had found a spent cartridge in Lennie Dunn's garden. Lawton did not cross-examine him.

There was a short adjournment. There would have been some sensation in court afterwards, as a screen had been erected in front of the witness box. Now came the Crown's star witness, Donald Caston (giving his evidence as 'Raycaston' as per his statement). He testified from behind the screen, so that the general public, but apparently not the jury, were prevented from seeing him. Donald was in military uniform, and handcuffed. When his name was called, his military escorts took off his handcuffs and he entered the witness box.[28]

He proceeded to give evidence largely as in his statements. Again, he mentioned meeting with Peter on 28 June, the day of the crime, rather than on the following day. He said that Peter had met him in the pub, taken him aside, and told him that he (Peter) had shot 'a young girl.' Donald claimed that while he had told Peter he had read the papers (about the shooting) he had not actually done so. Donald's response had been to call Peter 'a bloody liar.' Donald said that Peter then asked if he (Peter) could borrow some money, about five pounds. This was a big sum to Donald, as he said in evidence: 'The money he asked for I had not seen such money.' Donald was hazy about whether or not he had met Peter on

---

[28] *Daily Express*, 26 September 1945. The article does not name him, no doubt so as not to prejudice his possible upcoming court martial for desertion.

either of the two following days, but accepted meeting him on the Sunday.

On the Sunday, he related, he got in about midnight and met Peter. Dunn had been in the house as well. Peter had shown Donald the gun, although Donald 'did not think' Dunn had been present then. Peter had showed him the pistol. Peter had shown him the magazine and cartridges, and ejected a cartridge from the breech block. The gun was now shown to Donald in the witness box, and he identified it.

Then Donald told the crucial account:

Donald: ..he told me how he shot the young girl.

Byrne: Will you speak quite slowly and tell [the judge] and the jury what he said to you?

D: He said she was counting some money out [...] And he said that he said to her 'I'll have that, sister,' and she told him not to be a silly boy, and he passed the revolver from his right hand to the left to collect the money and it went off.

B: Yes, what happened when it went off, did he say?

D: She fell and groaned, or she went down groaning, he just took the money and ran out.

B: After he had told you that [,] what happened about the revolver?

D: I cannot remember what happened.

B: Did you keep possession of it, or what happened to it?

D: Yes, I took it. [...]

B: Where did you take it?

D: Round to my friend's. [...]

Donald confirmed that he had later returned the gun to Peter, who had asked him if he had got the money. He stated that Peter had later put the gun up the chimney. The rest of his account was told in brief:

B: The next night, that is the 2nd July, did you speak to two police officers?

D: Yes.

B: When you got the revolver out of the chimney were there any bullets in it, cartridges in it? I cannot remember what happened to the bullets, I found them in the kitchen.

B: Just look at the Exhibit No 3, five live cartridges. Did you find them somewhere?

D: Yes.

B: Where did you find them?

D: ..[I]n the kitchen, ...[n]ear the table, [rolled up in a rag].

Mr Lawton then cross-examined Donald. Again, he took a soft approach, rather than accuse the witness of lying. First he tried a small detail.

L: Let me just read to you [...] from your deposition. Do not think that I am suggesting that you are deliberately lying [...] but I am suggesting that with regard to the details of the conversation you may have just got a word here [or there] in a phrase wrong, you see what I mean?

D: Yes.

L: You see, according to your deposition, a copy of which I have got before me, when you appeared before the [magistrates court] you appear to have said this: 'He said he had done it. I called him a silly bugger. I believed him.'

D: Well, I have not got such a good memory as all that.

Lawton then pressed home the advantage.

L: This is exactly what I thought. Does it come to this, that with some of the little details of the story you may, as a result of the passing of time, have got a little dull in your recollection?

D: Yes.

L: Now let me come to the detail which I suggest got a little dull. You remember a few moments ago telling [the court] this: 'He said that he passed the [pistol] from his right hand into his left to collect the money and it went off.'

D: Yes.

L: What I am going to suggest to you is this, that you have made a mistake about the

100

words 'to collect the money' and that is not what was said to you by [Peter?]

D: I think it was.

L: That what he was making clear to you was that the lady in the garage was laughing at him, that he passed the revolver from his right hand to his left, and that he was standing there with it in his left hand when it went off, and said nothing about collecting the money. Do you think that might be right?

D: I do not know, I cannot say.

Donald's evidence was at an end, and he was led away.

Mr Byrne stood and said, 'My Lord, that is the case for the Prosecution.'

Mr Lawton then called Peter to give evidence. The youth was led from the dock into the witness box, and sworn.

Peter confirmed that he had made a statement to the police. He agreed that the parts of it relating to the purchase of the pistol from a Canadian soldier, and that he had borrowed the money to buy it from Lennie Dunn's mother. Then came the part relating to the crime itself.

Lawton: Now I want you to come at once to the afternoon of Thursday the 28th June. That afternoon, is it true, as you say in your statement, that you went from Loughborough Junction to the vicinity of the garage?

Peter: Yes.

L: Had you got the revolver with you?

P: Yes.

L: Where were you carrying it?

P: In my overcoat pocket.

L: Was it loaded?

P: Yes.

L: Had it been loaded when you bought it?

A: It was loaded when I bought it, yes.

L: Is it also true, as you say in your statement, that you intended to use that revolver for the purpose of going to the garage and holding up whoever was there?

P: Yes.

Peter went on to confirm that he had entered the garage by the gates through which cars went.

L: There was the office door on your left as you went in?

P: Yes.

L: At the time where was the revolver?

P: Still in my pocket.

L: Did you go up to the door of the office?

P: Yes.

L: Did you open it?

P: I took the gun out and then opened [the door].

L: What did you do, if anything, about cocking the gun?

P: I walked into the office and the woman was counting out money. I said 'I'll have that, sister.' She looked at me and said 'Don't be silly,' and I then cocked the gun.

Sir Ernest Charles, the judge at Peter's trial (National Portrait Gallery)

Mr Justice Charles now made the first of many interventions in Peter's evidence.

Judge: Why?

P: To eject a full bullet.

Judge: To do what?

P: To let out a full bullet.

L: Why did you touch the gun at all after the woman had said 'Don't be silly'?

P: To frighten her.

104

L: When you went into the office with the gun out as you have described to the Court, in which hand had you got it?

P: In my right hand.

L: We know from what you have just told us that you touched the gun, and you have given your reason for doing so. As a result of touching the gun, trying to carry out the operation which you did, did you change the gun from one hand to the other?

P: Yes.

L: What did you say to her?

P: 'This ain't no toy.'

Here the judge interrupted again, for no other apparent reason than to seek to correct Peter's grammar.

Judge: What?

P: 'This isn't no toy.'

L: What did she say, if anything?

P: She just looked at me in scorn like and said 'Don't be absurd.'

Judge: I did not catch you?

P: She looked at me as if to say 'Run away, little boy, and don't be absurd.'

L: When she said that had you still got the gun in your left hand?

P: Yes.

L: Was it a scornful remark she made?

P: Yes.

L: What effect did her scorn have upon you?

P: As if 'run away, I am not interested,' and then I did not know what to do. Then I tried to frighten her, and she just said 'Run away.'

L: She was not apparently in any way disturbed by your threats and your attempts to frighten her, was she?

P: No; as a matter of fact, when I first walked in and said 'I'll have that, sister' she carried on writing a bit more, and then she put down the pen and looked up.

L: Had you anticipated that your attempts to frighten a woman would lead to scorn and laughter at your expense?

P: No.

L: It was not quite what you had anticipated would happen, was it?

P: No, I did not expect anything like that.

L: What effect did it have upon you; what did you decide to do?

P: I did not know what to do, and I was thinking what to do when the gun went off.

L: Had you, or had you not, intended to pull the trigger?

P: No, sir.

L: On to the time when the gun went off had you put out your hand, or made any other attempt at movement, to get the money?

P: No.

L: Whereabouts were you standing when the gun went off?

P: I [had gone] in and closed the door behind me, and I was standing against the door.

L: And she was standing, was she not, by the cash desk?

P: Round the side of the cash desk.

L: What effect had the going off of the gun upon you?

P: I did not believe I had done it at first, I was standing there still, like, dazed like, and I see the woman falling. I saw the gun, I looked at the gun and it had been shot back and it had not cocked again properly, the empty shell had not jumped out, it was still in there, and the gun was half open, and I realised I had shot the woman, and I just turned round and grabbed a pile of the notes and ran out.

L: Why did you grab the pile of notes?

Judge: That is what you had come in there for, was not it, to get the money?

P: Yes.

L: And so you carried out the complete theft?

P: It was in the back of my mind, I just carried it on.

L: Let me just go back, Jarmain, over the ground you have covered so far in your evidence. We know that you went there with a revolver?

P: Yes.

Judge: So as to make you give her the money?

P: Yes.

L: Did you, or did you not, intend to fire the revolver at her if she refused to give you the money?

P: I did not intend to fire the revolver.

L:We know that you grabbed the money and rushed out of the office. Then you take the route which is set out in the statement that you gave to the police [..]?

P: Yes.

Following in detail the journey which is set out in that statement?

P: Yes.

L: And is the rest of your statement which deals with what happened afterwards about hiding the revolver, disposing of the ammunition and so on, true?

P: Yes.

Mr Lawton sat down. Laurence Byrne rose to cross-examine Peter. His courtroom style was later to be described as 'invariably polite and seldom raising his voice,' but it was also said that 'his powers of cross-examination [made] him a formidable opponent.'[29]

His first few questions simply established that Peter was short of money and had bought the gun in order to commit a robbery. Peter also confirmed that he had known the garage at Thornton Heath and knew something about it from a friend who used to work there.

---

[29] The Times, 2 November 1965.

Byrne: Then on 28 June […] you went [to the garage] with the revolver, is that right?

Peter: Yes.

B: With the intention of using the revolver in order to frighten somebody so that they would hand over their money to you?

P: Yes.

B: Did you know how the revolver worked?

P: Yes.

B: Did you know how to load and unload it?

P: Yes.

B: When you went to the garage was the revolver loaded?

P: Yes.

B: Had you any intention of firing it?

P: No.

B: Why was it loaded then?

P: That was the way I bought it.

B: The way you bought it? Why take the weapon to the garage loaded if you only intended brandishing it in order to frighten the person for the money?

P: I do not know.

B: You do not know?

P: No.

B: When you walked in through the door of the office, was the revolver in such a condition that if you pulled the trigger it would fire?

P: No.

B: What had you to do in order to make it ready for firing by pulling the trigger?

P: Cock it.

[...]

B: Did you then change it over to the other hand?

P: No.

B: When did you change it from one hand to the other?

P: I changed it from my right hand to my left to cock it.

B: And then you kept it in your left hand afterwards, did you?

P: Yes.

B: Was that in order to take the money with your right hand?

P: No.

B: Just tell me this: the weapon must have been pointing at Mrs Phillips, must not it?

P: Yes.

B: Did you know that?

P: I knew it was pointing towards her, yes.

B: You knew it was. You intended it to point at her, did you?

P: Yes.

B: And you know, did you, when it was pointing at her that if you pulled the trigger she would be shot?

P: Yes.

B:Was it then that you said 'This is not a toy?'

P: After I cocked it, yes.

B: She was very brave, was not she?

P: Yes.

B: She said 'Don't be absurd,' you say?

P: Yes.

B: How did the revolver come to be discharged after that?

P: Well, I was standing with it in my left hand and she said 'Don't be absurd,' and I was trying to think what else I could do, whether I should run out of the office, or grab some money and run out.

Judge: That is not quite what you are asked, you know. How did this revolver, which you knew was in such a condition that if you pulled the trigger – it was pointing at this woman and she would be shot – how did you come to squeeze the trigger so that she was shot?

P: I do not know.

B: You say, after she had said 'Don't be absurd' you were considering how you could get away?

P: Yes, whether she would-

B: Are you telling the Jury that while you were considering how you could get away you were still pointing the loaded revolver at the woman?

P: Yes.

B: With your finger on the trigger?

P:The way I was holding it, yes.

B: It must have been, must not it?

P: Yes.

B: And she was shot?

P: Yes.

B: I suppose you were horror-struck at that, were you?

P: Yes.

B: Why did you take the money?

P: That is what I went there for.

B: What you went there for, yes. You were not so horrified that you forgot to take the money, were you?

P: No – yes, I was horrified, I was frightened, but I knew I went there for money, and I turned round and took it.

B: You still remembered, although this woman was then, you say, on the ground and groaning, was not she?

P: She was falling.

B: You knew you had shot her?

P: I realised that, yes.

B: And although there she was falling, you having shot her, you still remembered that you had gone there to take the money?

P: Yes.

B: And you took it?

P: Yes.

Mr Byrne had no more questions, and Peter was returned to the dock.

Mr Lawton stood up. He would have known how uncompromising Mr Justice Charles had been in his summing-up in Hulten and Jones's case. In that matter, the judge had said that 'even if the shot was fired in the midst of a commission of a felony and in order to frighten,' it would still be murder. Lawton hoped that the judge would be able to indicate at this stage whether he would direct the jury that a manslaughter verdict was possible. 'My Lord,' he asked, 'that is the case for the defence. Might I have your Lordship's ruling as to the verdict which I can ask the jury to come to?'

'I cannot tell you that,' replied Mr Justice Charles. 'You must address the Jury, and I shall tell the jury what the law is, you know.'

Mr Lawton then addressed the jury. His closing speech was not noted in the transcript, so we only have the press reports to go on. He praised Mrs Phillips's bravery, saying 'Hers is a story of courage which probably has not been surpassed. He was acting like an American gangster. He pointed a revolver at her and used the words of gangsterism, and she calmly went on writing...He expected her to be a cowering woman, and found a woman of scorn.' Speaking of his young client he said 'I put him before you as a stupid, vicious youth, but not a hardened criminal,' and having had no intention to kill when he went to the garage. He urged the jury to return a verdict of manslaughter, on the basis that Peter had given up the plan of robbery at the time the gun had gone off.[30]

When Mr Lawton sat down, the judge asked Mr Byrne if he wanted to make a closing speech. The latter complained that Lawton had addressed the jury first when he, Byrne, should have done so. But Byrne indicated that unless the judge specifically requested it, he would not address the jury. Mr Justice Charles then proceeded to sum up the case.

The judge started by stating: '[T]his is, of course, the most serious type of case that any jury can be called upon to consid-

---

[30] *Croydon Advertiser,* 28 September 1945, *Morning Advertiser,* 26 September 1945.

er, it is a charge of murder..' He went on to state that the burden of proof was on the prosecution, who had to prove the case beyond a reasonable doubt. He then went on to comment on the defence case.

'..Mr Lawton, who has addressed you, if I may say so, with great skill and propriety on behalf of the accused, does not for one moment invite you to find a verdict of not guilty, that could not be. What he does is to invite you to find a verdict not of murder but of manslaughter.' He proceeded to state the felony-murder rule, and the law that a death caused by an offence less than felony would be manslaughter.

He continued, referring closely to Peter's own evidence. 'This man was, by all admissions, by his own sworn testimony, engaged upon an armed robbery, and that is a felony and nothing but a felony, and in the course of that armed felony this unfortunate young woman met her death at his hands. You have been invited to say that there was a sort of break, that is to say, that when this woman refused to be cowed by the exhibition of this loaded and cocked revolver this man was so bewildered with her bravery that he forgot and set aside the executing of the felony for which he had entered the garage, and that while momentarily, almost, he was he was in that condition of mind he inadvertently, he knows not how, squeezed the trigger and [...][injured her so that she died a little time afterwards.' Now, I find it very difficult in directing you that you can consider any such proposition.'

The judge went through Peter's evidence in great detail, in particular:

'So that he entered that garage to rob, he had a loaded revolver which he cocked, to assist him as part of the paraphernalia of the robbery; he kept it pointed towards the body of that unfortunate woman while she was disputing his right to the money, and after he had shot her down, and after she lay groaning on the ground, instead of going to her assistance, if the mischance had happened that Mr Lawton would have you believe had happened, he executed the purpose for which he went to the garage, he stole the money, and so the crime was executed, and in the course of the execution that woman met her death.'

The judge continued in this vein, and later said:

'It may well be that he did not intend or desire that revolver to go off. I have to tell you that that does not make any difference: if you accept the circumstances under which this terrible killing took place, that is murder, plain, simple murder.'

Lastly, he emphasised that the jury could only return verdicts of murder or manslaughter, not a verdict of not guilty to any offence.

The jury retired to consider their verdict. It was now early evening, sometime between six and seven. Peter was taken back to the court cells while the jury deliberated. He would have been told by his solicitors or his barrister that the longer the jury were out for, the better his chance of an acquittal or a retrial. At that time, jury verdicts had to be unanimous – if the jury were unable to reach such a verdict, the defendant would probably have to face a second trial. In the event he was brought back up swiftly. The jury had only been out for eleven minutes.

The clerk of the court asked, 'Members of the jury, are you agreed upon your verdict?'

The jury foreman replied, 'We are.'

'Do you find the prisoner, Peter Joseph Jarmain, guilty or not guilty of murder?'

'Guilty.'

'You find him guilty of murder, and that is the verdict of you all?'

'Yes.'

The clerk then addressed Peter: 'Prisoner at the bar, you stand convicted of murder. Have you anything to say why the court should not give you judgement of death according to law?'

Peter replied, 'No, sir.'

He would have already been told what the procedure would be, that the sentence of death was automatic and that nothing would alter it. Most prisoners in that situation made no response. At a treason trial thirty years earlier, the prisoner, Sir Roger Casement, had responded to the query with a lengthy speech questioning the justice of his prosecution and conviction.[31] Sentence of death, and ultimately execution, had duly followed.

An usher then read out the proclamation, 'charging and commanding all manner of persons to keep silence while sentence of death was being passed upon the prisoner at the bar, upon pain of imprisonment.' The black cap – a square of black cloth which was, and indeed still is, part of a judge's full formal attire – was placed upon the judge's wig.

Mr Justice Charles said to the young defendant:

'Peter Joseph Jarmain, you have been found guilty on the very clearest
evidence possible of the murder of this unfortunate woman. My duty is to pass the sentence of the court upon you, and that is

---

[31] *The Black Diaries of Roger Casement*, Maurice Girodias, Grove Press 1959.

that you will be taken hence to the prison in which you were last confined and from there to a place of execution where you will be hanged by the neck until you are dead and thereafter your body buried within the precincts of the prison, and may the Lord have mercy upon your soul.'

A chaplain, seated near the judge, responded 'Amen.'

That Friday's *Croydon Advertiser*, reporting the scene, reminded the readers that Peter was standing in the same dock where William Joyce had stood days before, and indicated that Peter was impassive as Joyce had been, when sentence was passed. The article reported that a woman was heard sobbing quietly at the back of the court. The following day's *Daily Mirror* described Peter at his sentencing as looking 'even younger than his eighteen years' when sentence was passed. He was said to look '[p]ale faced [...] with a lock of hair falling boyishly over his forehead'.

`Chapter Five: This Lonely Cell

Peter was taken down to the cells, and shortly afterwards driven away to prison. His status had changed considerably. From being just one more remand prisoner, he was now a convicted man, furthermore, one awaiting execution. His destination clearly indicated that. He had been driven to court from Brixton Prison, which did not have, and had never had, a gallows. Now, he was on his way to Wandsworth Prison, which did have such equipment, and where two men had already been hanged that year.

Only days after his sentence was passed, the Prison Commissioners sent a memorandum to the governor of Wandsworth Prison advising them of the steps to be taken regarding Peter's proposed execution. The proposed date was fixed for 16 October 1945. The Commissioners proposed that Henry Critchell might be suitable as assistant executioner. They did not propose anyone for the role of 'lead' executioner. That task, in London's prisons at least, usually went to Albert Pierre point, son of a previous hangman and nephew of a then-current one.

The memorandum went into a lot of detail on what was expected to happen on the morning of the execution. The sentence was expected to be carried out at eight in the morning, the usual hour. If, however, it took place at nine o'clock, then 'prisoners were expected to be 'scattered about the prison at their respective tasks,' such that any noise caused by the trap doors 'should pass unnoticed.' The clock chime would be silenced so the prisoners would not be aware of the exact time of the hanging taking place. If any young prisoners, in the Governor's opinion, would be distressed by the forthcoming execution they were to be considered for transfer to another prison.

The battle to save Peter's life started almost immediately, led by his mother and his brother Sydney. They gave an interview to the *Croydon Advertiser* - it appeared in the same issue which reported the sentencing. Sydney related Peter's medical history, and summed it up by saying that Peter had

'Never had much of a life.'[32]. Sydney also spoke of Peter's leaving school to support his mother, and of his doing fire-watching duties during the Blitz despite his disability.

Sydney went on to say that a chance meeting on VE day had led to Peter moving with a set of other boys, and that he (Sydney) was convinced that his younger brother was led astray. It seemed that the family blamed Peter's meeting with Caston for his predicament.

Peter, he said, had never been in trouble before and was well liked by their neighbours. Mrs Jarmain mentioned that he had stayed out late at times, but she had not worried about this as he was 'always considerate and well behaved at home.'

Mother and brother took the view that Peter's character was shown by a letter he had written the day before his trial. Presumably they received it either before setting off for court on the day of the trial, or on their return.

---

[32] This line was used as the headline in the paper

The letter was published with the article, and reads:

"Brixton, 24.9.45

My dear Mum,

Just a few lines to say I am very sorry for all the worry I have caused you. Please forgive me, Mum, you know I wouldn't kill anyone for the world.

Take care of yourself and don't worry about me. If you are OK, I will be happy.

This time next week, I expect I will be gone from here. Keep your fingers crossed.

This is about all for the moment. Cheerio for now. Take care of the livestock. God bless you, Mum.

Your ever-loving son,

PETE."

The article concluded by stating that a petition was being organised with a view to a reprieve being granted. Arguably this was a premature step. Some people, it is true, never appealed their convictions but simply petitioned the Home Secretary for a reprieve (or indeed accepted their fate and did not even do that). However the majority of people convicted of murder appealed to the Court of Criminal Appeal. That court could overturn the verdict and either acquit Peter completely or reduce the conviction to one of manslaughter. If the murder conviction stood, then so would the sentence of death, subject to any decision to the contrary by the Home Secretary.

Notice of appeal was submitted by Peter's solicitors on 27 September, just two days after the conviction. Strictly speaking this was 'an application for leave to appeal,' a distinction which will be explained later. The application seems to have had one practical effect. Peter was moved from Wandsworth Prison the following morning, to Wormwood Scrubs Prison north of the river, in Hammersmith and Fulham. [Another possible reason for the move might have been the fact that Frederick Lawton's father William was governor at Wandsworth. It might have been thought unseemly for the defence barrister's father to potentially have to supervise a prisoner's exe-cution].Once again, he was away from the grim presence of the apparatus of death, as his new home, 'The Scrubs', also did not have a gallows. However, officialdom was still planning for the possibility of events taking such a turn. The letter from the Gov-ernor of Wormwood Scrubs to the Home Secretary, dated 28 September, acknowledg-ing Peter's arrival there, contains the omi-nous paragraph:

"He will remain in my custody until the eve of his execution, when he will be transferred to Pentonville Prison."

Elsewhere in London, another eigh-teen year old was pondering his fate. Both sets of German prisoners of war had now been tried by military tribunals - similar to courts martial - for the murder of fellow POWs. The trials had taken place at a mili-tary detention centre at 8 Kensington Palace Gardens, known as 'the London Cage,' where the prisoners were being held along with some other prisoners due to give evidence.

The first trial was of the eight men accused of the Comrie killing – four more suspects had been discharged just before the trial. The trial started on 2 July 1945, and continued for some days. The defendants spoke little or no English, and so the proceedings had to be translated for them. Only news organisations that agreed not to publicise the names of other prisoners giving evidence against the defendants, were allowed to follow this trial, and that of the Sheffield prisoners.

The procedure was like that at a court martial. The panel – the judges who would decide guilt or innocence- was made up of a presiding officer, a colonel, and five other officers. A legally trained person, the Judge Advocate, was on hand to make legal rulings to guide the panel. The prosecuting and defending advocates were all British officers, who were solicitors or barristers in civilian life. One of the defence advocates, Captain Roger Willis, had been a prisoner of war himself, having not long returned from German captivity. A number of prisoners gave evidence about seeing the deceased being attacked, beaten and then dragged to be hanged from the pipe. They were all cross-examined by officers representing the prisoners, but to little effect.

One of the defendants was discharged at the end of the prosecution case, as the court accepted that there was not sufficient evidence against him. The remaining prisoners gave evidence, and for the most part condemned themselves by stating that they felt that the killing was justified to punish a traitor, even if they did not admit their own actions in striking the fatal blows. Some accepted that they had taken part in hanging the (probably dead) body of Rosterg. At the end of the trial one man was acquitted and six found guilty.[33] All six of those convicted – Zuhlsdorff, Bruling, Pallme Koenig, Mertens, Hertzig and Goltz - were sentenced to death.

The trial of the prisoners accused of the Sheffield camp killing opened at the same centre, on 8 August.

Eighteen-year-old Armin Kühne was on trial along with Emil Schmittendorf,

---

[33] *For Fuhrer and Fatherland*, Roderick de Normann (1996) The History Press

Heinz Ditzler and Jürgen Kersting, for the murder of Rettig at Lodge Moor camp.[34] By then Armin may have heard ominous news. His family's home town of Schwerin, occupied by the Americans and later the British since May, had now been handed over to the forces of the communist Soviet Union. The Western Allies had withdrawn to a line along the Elbe River, separating the Soviet from the Western-occupied parts of Germany. This was part of a wider division of Western and communist spheres of influence, along a barrier which would become known as the 'Iron Curtain.' Communism, loathed by the Nazis, had now come to rule over Armin's nearest and dearest. He wrote to his family, probably having no idea whether the letters would get through.

"I did not hear from you since one year [ago]," he wrote. "I have been in captivity since 8 October 1944 and since 24 March 1945 I have been accused of murder. On the 7th August my fate will be decided. If I should not be able to return home, don't

---

[34] Ditzler and Schmittendorf had briefly escaped not long after the murder.

take it too badly.I have risked my life for the fatherland have given my blood for my comrades and have I remained a German and shall remain that to the end. One thing I know, it is only because I am a Nazi and non-Nazis accuse me. They are also Germans. You, my dear parents, must know that I am innocent. I have suffered enough and Manfred has had to give his life for Germany, so I can do it as well.(..) I don't mind to go for you and the liberty of our fatherland.

I greet you from England

Your little son

Armin."

Kühne and Schmittendorf were accused of being the ringleaders of the assault. Emil Schmittendorf was a 31 year old *feldwebel* or sergeant-major. Proceedings unfolded with similar procedure to the earlier trial. The defences were factual, each prisoner seeking to argue that he had not struck any blows – or at least no fatal ones – against Rettig in the melee. In the run-up to the trial some of the defendants , including

Kühne, had sent notes to possible witnesses suggesting that they give evidence exonerating the writer of the notes. One such note was put in evidence against Kühne, who rejected the claim that it implicated him further.[35]

The authorities contested – and the press reported – that Armin was twenty-one. In his closing speech on 13 August, Armin's advocate, Lieutenant Brands[36] gave a summary of Armin's life stating that owing to the prisoner's intensive Nazi Youth training, he had left home at twelve, had not seen his parents since, and was eighteen. On that same day, the court returned its verdict. The conflicting evidence from and about the prisoners had some effect – Ditzler and Kersting were found not guilty. However Armin and Schmittendorf were found guilty and

---

[35] While a full transcript of the trial is not available, chapter 4 of Sophie Jackson's book *Churchill's Unexpected Guests*, previously cited, provides a fairly detailed account.

[36] Reported in the *Manchester Guardian* (now *The Guardian*) 14 August 1945.

duly sentenced to death.[37] In due course all the condemned men were removed to Kempton Park, a peacetime racecourse then being used as a prisoner of war camp.

Following his sentence, Armin wrote – presumably to his parents:

"It has to be. HEIL YOU. Death sentence."

A few quirks of law have to be explained here. With a civilian trial, when someone was convicted and sentenced these matters could be published immediately. The conviction and sentence would stand unless overturned on appeal. However with courts martial and military tribunals a different system applied. Acquittals could be reported at once. However when someone was convicted and sentenced, the press would only report that (in the words of the *Manchester Guardian* on Kühne and Schmittendorf) 'The findings of the court with regards to the other defendants [...] will be made known later.' This was be-

---

[37] *Murder, Mutiny and the Military: British Court Martial Cases, 1940 – 1966,* Gerry R Rubin, Francis Boutle Publishers, 2005.

cause neither the conviction nor the sentence of a court martial or military tribunal was final until confirmed. The military authority which had summoned the matter for trial would have to review the court's findings. They could confirm conviction and sentence, or confirm conviction but alter sentence. Also they could quash conviction and sentence, in which case the defendant would return to their prison camp or barracks as before.

This was a major difference between Armin's case and that of Peter. The British public knew Peter's age, and that he had been convicted of murder and sentenced to hang. On the other hand, not only had most of the public been misled as to Armin's age, they did not even know that he had been convicted at all, much less sentenced to death. Those familiar with court martial procedure could have inferred this, but the great majority of newspaper readers would probably not have such knowledge.

Peter had an appeal in hand, but the public campaign for a possible reprieve, was still afoot. It was to hit the national papers.

Following the Friday's Croydon paper, the following day's *Daily Mirror* ran an article headlined **MOTHER IS TRYING TO SAVE HIM**, above a photo of Peter, sad-eyed and in a sharp suit. The article read, in full:

"This is eighteen-year-old Peter Jarmain, who is now lying in a London [prison] under sentence of death for the murder of a woman cashier whom he shot in a hold-up at a Thornton Heath, Surrey, garage.

Last night, his mother, a widow, living in Camberwell, started a fight to save him.

A petition for a reprieve was drawn up by Mr Victor Mishcon, a solicitor representing the family, the grounds for the plea being Jarmain's age, and the fact that 'he had no father to guide him.'

The youth's brother has been given compassionate leave from the Army in Germany to help with the petition, which has the support of the local MP, Lieutenant Colonel Lipton.

Jarmain was in hospital from the age of seven and in a cripples' school with a leg in irons till he was fifteen.[38]

His father died suddenly before he left school.

The woman shot by Jarmain told him 'run away little boy,' just before he squeezed the trigger."

Peter's picture in the *Mirror* article (Daily Mirror).

---

[38] This would seem to be in error based on what we already know.

Mishcon was a civil solicitor - his firm had not acted for Peter at his trial, nor would they on the appeal. He had founded his own law firm in Brixton eight years beforehand, when he was only twenty-two. He had served in the army during the war, rising to the rank of major. He had been elected to Lambeth Borough Council on his return from war service, and represented the Angell Ward. He may well have been Mrs Jarmain's local councillor as that ward straddled Brixton and Camberwell.

Another, even more flamboyant character also entered the campaign. He was Basil St John Eagan, and described himself as a youth worker.[39] On 1 October, he addressed a letter to the Home Secretary. It was described as a 'petition,' but not in the sense of a list of signatures. The letter was addressed to 'His Excellency the Secretary of State', Basil being fond of high-flown phrases.

---

[39] The author has been able to find out little about him other than to confirm his address at the time. His dates of birth, and presumed death, are elusive. It maybe that he had changed, or at least altered, his name.

In the letter Basil asked for a meeting with the Home Secretary, to seek clemency for Peter, 'the above-mentioned boy now lying under sentence of death in Wormwood Scrubs.' He stressed Peter's age, his 'lack of fatherly control,' his previous excellent behaviour, his 'unhappy childhood as a cripple', and his 'devotion to his widowed mother,' and lastly his lack of intent to kill. It ended with the clearly inaccurate flourish, 'Peter Joseph Jarmain is not a criminal.'

Basil stated that he had known Peter for a long time, being a voluntary youth worker 'among crippled youth' in conjunction with the charitable Shaftesbury Society.

A few days later, Basil wrote to the Home Secretary again. His letter was addressed in the same quaint style, starting 'I am obliged to submit to Your Excellency the enclosed document.' However the contents of this enclosure were more controversial than the preceding one.

Solicitor Victor Mishcon, in 1951. (National Portrait Gallery)

In the document, Basil made a number of allegations against Peter's solicitors and the police. He accused the former of not properly defending Peter – specifically he alleged that a solicitor, Rawllence, had told Basil over the telephone that he (the solicitor) 'had no time to visit Wormwood Scrubs.' The reference to 'the Scrubs' rather than Brixton must indicate that the discussions related to the appeal rather than the trial. In any event as we shall see the appeal would turn on points of law from the trial, and was thus mostly in the hands of Mr Lawton, the barrister. He would not have needed to take any more instructions from Peter.

The allegations against the police were something of a high-stakes gamble at a time when the police were generally held in high regard. In short Basil accused the police of 'conspiring' with an army deserter to 'unlawfully' gain entry to the Luxor Street house on the night of Peter's being taken away by the police. Basil also alleged the prosecution had put forward Peter's statement in court 'knowing it to be false in substance and in fact.'

More alarmingly, he alleged that the police had failed to interrogate or apprehend two persons who were, he wrote, openly boasting of their complicity in the 'hold-up' and shooting at the Red Arrow Garage. He went on to claim that Inspector Bastable had ignored a relevant letter sent to him in July, and that there were witnesses who would support his, Basil's, assertions.

Bastable may have thought that his involvement in the case was largely at an end, but was now called upon to rely to the allegations. Of course claims about the actions or inaction of Peter's lawyers, did not concern him. But in a reply to his superiors, he stated that the police had not known of Caston's status as a deserter when he made his statement to them or when he retrieved the gun from the house. As we know, the police were able to enter the house without being let in. Nowadays the question of how lawful the police entry to the building was, might be of importance. However in 1945, these matters would not have affected any court's decisions as to Peter's guilt or innocence.

The Inspector also replied as to his discussions with Dunn, and that there was no evidence of his or any other person's involvement in the crime. Also, Bastable asserted that Peter's statement had been voluntarily made. This was of course borne out by the fact that Peter's case in court had not deviated that much from his statement. Lastly, Bastable denied ever receiving any letter in July as mentioned.

Basil – and mention of Dunn – was to crop up yet again. A week or so later, Basil visited Peter in prison. Privacy in a prison was, and is, never absolute. A prison officer overheard part of their discussions, by accident or design. He reported to the prison governor, and the details were ultimately brought to Inspector Bastable who had to reply yet again.

Mr Farthing, the officer, noted that during the visit, Basil had said 'I admire you, having the guts to take all the blame and not give away the two others who were with you at the time.' Allegedly Basil had gone on to say 'I am making a full investigation, and I spoke to Mrs Dunn about her son being involved in it, and she said "I don't care if they hang Peter Jarmain, I am going to defend my son for all I am worth."'

Bastable, no doubt wearily, responded to his superiors that he had interviewed Dunn twice, and that the young man had initially denied all knowledge, but later given an account similar to Peter's. He stressed that as Peter was in custody by then he and Dunn could not have aligned their stories. As to the allegation of Dunn's involvement Bastable wrote, 'From this it will be seen that although it is possible that Dunn and some other person were in some way concerned with the murder of Mrs Phillips, there is not a tittle of evidence to support this.'

Meanwhile, there had been developments with the first set of German prisoners at Kempton Park. The first group of prisoners, those convicted of the Perth killing, had their conviction confirmed on 23 July. It seems this happened in a two-stage process. First the conviction and sentence were confirmed, by the army's chief legal officer, the Justice Advocate General, holding that the men had admitted involvement in the lynching of Rosterg and that they had not been entitled to take the law into their own hands.[40] While this decision was not formally declared to those affected until much later, it would seem that they were told of it. Afterwards, they had the opportunity to make representations seeking a reprieve. It is not clear how many of them sought

---

[40] de Normann, work previously cited p 158

clemency, but one, Hertzig, was successful. His sentence was reduced to one of fifteen years' imprisonment, to be served in a civil prison. It is not known what grounds he advanced. He was at least as guilty as most of the others, having kicked Rosterg and dragged his body away to be strung up. However, for whatever reasons, the military authorities decided that he was to be spared. Maybe they decided that six executions would be too much on one occasion. Or maybe they felt that even without Herzig they had enough people to create a supposed deterrent effect.

British military executions were often carried out by firing squad, particularly in the field. However, at home, the method was often hanging. The British military did not have a prison with execution facilities.[41] On 5 October, the five unfortunate prisoners were driven from Kempton Park camp to HMP Pentonville. They were accompanied by military escorts.

---

[41] Unlike the US military, which during WW2 used the former British civil prison of Shepton Mallett in Somerset.

The following morning the *Times* published a brief notice indicating that the five men had been convicted by a military court and that their convictions and sentences having been confirmed, they were to be hanged that morning. This would have been the first the general public would have known of their convictions, much less their imminent executions. Later that morning the men were executed over a two-hour period by executioner Albert Pierrepoint, and his assistants Stephen Wade and Harry B Allen. Two of the men – Breuling and Mertens – were twenty-one, the others were all aged twenty.

Although Peter was not in a prison with a gallows, he would have been detained under the same system in force in such places. He would have been in solitary confinement, with little or no contact with other prisoners. He would have been in the care of a group of prison officers, called 'Capital Charge Officers,' often volunteers from other prisons.[42] There would normally be eight officers, six of them doing shifts

42 Capital Punishment UK website.
  https://www.capitalpunishmentuk.org/

two at a time so the prisoner was never alone. This was – in part at least - to prevent the prisoner taking his or her own life. The two officers who did not do a shift (and therefore who the prisoner had never met) would be with the executioner on the final morning, for the condemned person's walk to the gallows.

The prison doctor might allocate the convict a special diet if they were (unsurprisingly) eating little. Force feeding could be authorised. Dr Grierson had ordered such a course of action against the Indian assassin Udham Singh in 1940, when the latter went on hunger strike.[43] The prisoner's weight would be monitored regularly, for reasons which shall become clear later. Uniquely among prisoners, condemned convicts were allowed a ration of beer.

Condemned prisoners were allowed newspapers, although with any references to their own case cut out. However, details of other criminal matters would not be re-

[43] *The Patient Assassin* by Anita Anand, Simon and Schuster 2019. Singh had killed the former British governor he held responsible for the Amritsar massacre of 1919.

moved. Peter would probably have heard of the multiple execution at Pentonville. He would almost certainly have reflected that the men had all been very young, and had died on the same gallows that would claim his own life if the worst happened.

Today's readers in Western countries will probably base most of their knowledge of capital punishment on what they see or read about that process in the present-day United States. They may think that similar things happened in Britain in Peter's day, and in many cases they would be wrong. British prisons did not have a 'death row' with dozens of prisoners under sentence of death. This was in part because several prisons up and down England and Wales had their own execution facilities, while in the US most states had many prisons, but only carried out executions in one. Also, the appeal system in the US was (and is) complicated. A prisoner could appeal against their conviction in an array of state and federal courts, seeking stays of execution at all these levels. In England and Wales, most prisoners only had one appeal avenue, two if the right of petition to the Home Secretary was included. The record period spent in the condemned cell had been four months in the then-recent case of Antonio 'Babe' Mancini. He was a gangster of Italian origin who in May 1941 had fatally stabbed an opponent in the shoulder during a fight in a nightclub. Mancini appealed to the Court of Criminal Appeal, and having failed there, secured the permission needed to appeal to the highest court, the House of Lords. After the dismissal of that appeal, Mancini's luck ran out in October that year. He became Albert Pierrepoint's first subject as lead executioner.[44]

Had the murder taken place forty years earlier there would only have been the Home Secretary possibly standing between Peter and the gallows. The Court of Criminal Appeal had only existed since 1907.

However there was a crucial difference between the Court of Criminal Appeal and its civil equivalent, the Court of Appeal. The latter was made up of specialised ap-

---

[44] *Hanged at Pentonville*, Steve Fielding, The History Press 2008.

peal judges, who had already done their time trying civil cases. They had become 'Lord Justices of Appeal.' They could make decisions independently of worrying how allowing an appeal would affect their relationship with the judges whose decision they might overrule. But the Court of Criminal Appeal was made up entirely of judges who still sat as trial judges in criminal matters. Very few appeals turned on factual issues – most of them related to whether the judge's summing up had been correct. Appeals tended to be dismissed, judges frequently stating in their appeal judgments that 'no fault [was] to to be found with this impeccable summing-up.'[45]

Peter may have been looking forward to seeing and hearing his appeal. Most prisoners would have liked to be present – it was their only chance of seeing any part of the remaining legal process. But many convicts went to the gallows never seeing their appeals being argued in court. This was because their barristers first had to apply to the judges for 'leave' (permission) to ap-

---

[45] David Yallop, *To Encourage The Others* 1971, [Constable, 2014].

peal, and this took place in the prisoner's absence. The appeal judges could – and often did – declare that they would treat the application for leave as the appeal itself. The prisoner's barrister would then have to deliver his appeal argument, and the prosecution would make their full response. The appeal would be resolved – more often dismissed – on the same day. The judges might give their full reasons on a later date, but the prisoner would not be present for that.

Peter's application for leave to appeal was heard on 16 October. The Court of Criminal Appeal sat at the Royal Court of Justice in the Strand. It is only about seven miles from the Old Bailey, and is a large, impressive Victorian Gothic building, built in the 1870s and opened in 1882. It is near St Clement's Dane church, at that time heavily damaged by air raids.

Over the porches leading into the Royal Courts are impressive statues – a figure of Jesus, one of King Solomon, and one of King Alfred the Great, also one of Moses. These all figures of persons reputed to be wise, fair and just. However over the judge's entrance are images representing perhaps a more realistic take on what went on in the building. These are images of a cat and a dog, representing litigants in court. Frederick Lawton must have been prepared to fight a cat-and-dog struggle to protect Peter's interests, and hopefully to save his life.

The principal actors took their places in one of the oak-panelled courtrooms. Once again, Lawton was pitted against Laurence Byrne. The three judges filed in. Heading the panel was Sir Frederic Wrottesley. He sat between Sir Wintringham Stable and Sir George Lynskey. While not heaving, the public gallery would have had a smattering of attenders. Doubtless Peter's close relatives would have been there, along with some journalists and maybe some members of the public drawn by the morbid drama of watching a man's life being decided upon.

The judges indicated that they would hear the application for leave as the appeal itself. As he represented the appellant, Lawton rose to his address the court first.

He argued that the trial judge's summing up was defective. This was of course, a high-stakes position to take. Lawton sought to draw a difference between a shot fired deliberately but unintentionally causing injury – a warning shot for example– and a shot fired entirely by accident. He contended that Peter 'was not guilty of murder unless he pulled the trigger voluntarily, and if his will did not go with the action of his finger, he was guilty of manslaughter only, and the jury should have been so directed.[46] He went on to say that 'Where death is due to a violent act, which was ... involuntary, the mere fact that the general design was that of a felony involving violence does not render a killing which occurred in the course of it murder.'

The judges called for the pistol, which had been kept as an exhibit. They examined it – apparently trying the trigger. Mr Justice Wrottesley – who had army experience from World War One - remarked that it needed a strong pull.[47]

---

[46] (1946) 31 Criminal Appeal Reports 39.

[47] *Croydon Advertiser* 19 October 1945.

Mr Byrne rose to respond. He said that the summing up had been correct, and that this was supported by the judgments in earlier cases, including both appeal judgments in Beard's case.

In cases where the judges had to have lengthy discussions about a decision, they would leave the courtroom to do so. In this case, they announced at the end of the barrister's speeches, that the appeal would be dismissed. They would give their reasons later. Lawton's job was over. The news would no doubt have been conveyed to Peter the same day. He, his family and supporters now knew that their only hope was for a reprieve from the Home Secretary.

The judges returned on the following Monday, to give their judgment in the case. They confirmed the existing law, ending with the following paragraph:

'We think that the object and scope of this branch of the law is at least this, that he who uses violent measures in the commission of a felony involving personal violence, does so at his own risk and is guilty of murder if those measures result inadvertently in the death of the victim. For this purpose, the use of a loaded firearm in order to frighten the person victimised into submission is a violent measure. The recent case of Hulten and Jones, [the 'Cleft Chin' case] decided in this court, is clear authority for this proposition.'

Others had already come to terms with the fact that their first avenue of appeal had come to a dead end. Emil and Armin had both petitioned the military authorities against their conviction and sentence. On 6 September, the General Officer Commanding the London District confirmed both decisions. The authorities had satisfied themselves as to some technical issues raised by the judge advocate as to the identification of the corpse. They had also confirmed that Armin was much younger than his stated age. While the military were not strictly bound by the prohibition on executing offenders under eighteen, they observed it in practice. Eventually they were satisfied that Armin was in fact eighteen, and therefore he could be made subject to capital punishment.[48]

Although this decision would fall to be formally announced to the two later, they would have been informed of it. The two soldiers seem to have reacted in different ways. Emil Schmittendorf, who was aged thirty-one, had been a professional soldier, having joined in 1934, the year after the Nazis had come to power. However his wife and children had apparently gone missing during the fighting around Berlin in the last days of the war in Europe. He seemed re-signed to his fate.[49]   Armin, however, was determined to fight for his life, and pre-pared to submit another petition.

---

[48] *Murder, Mutiny and the Military etc*, Gerry Rubin.

[49] *The March on London*, Charles Whiting.

Chapter Six: 'At Eighteen, A Boy Is Still A Child..'

Peter's fate was now in the hands of the Home Secretary. Monarchs up till William IV had sat in cabinet with their advisers, deciding which convicts should live and which should die. However with the young queen Victoria's accession to the throne in 1837, her prime minister Lord Melbourne thought it would be distasteful for an 18 year old woman to be involved in such decisions. From then on those weighty matters were part of the Home Secretary's job.[50] In practice, the senior civil servants made their recommendation to the Home Secretary who generally – but not always – followed their advice. If his decision was in favour of mercy, the Home Secretary would tender his recommendation to the King or Queen. The latter was bound by convention to accept the Secretary's advice, and would then alter the punishment to a sentence of imprisonment ('reprieving' the prisoner). If the decision was not in favour of mercy, the

[50] *With Malice Aforethought*, Louis Blom-Cooper, Terence Morris,Bloomsbury 2004.

monarch was not involved at all. The execution would follow without further authorisation.

Over the years, the custom arose of having the names and details of those under sentence of death, printed on a framed card placed in the Home Secretary's office. Dates of appeal, and of reprieve or execution, would be added to the card. In the 1930s, the then Home Secretary Sir John Simon had a Latin maxim engraved on the frame, *Nulla unquam de mortis hominis cuncutatio longa est* – a quotation from the Roman poet Juneval . The English translation of this is 'You can never hesitate too long before deciding that a man must die.'

One door to a potential reprieve had already slammed shut. Dr Grierson, having attended Peter's trial, had confirmed in writing to the prison governor (who would have notified the Home Secretary) that no issue of insanity had arisen during the trial. There was no question of a reprieve on mental health grounds.

The morning papers duly reported the dismissal of Peter's appeal on Wednesday 17

October 1945. Among the people reading this item was Mrs Grace Harrison, of Minehead in Somerset. She quickly put pen to paper, and hers may have been the first letter received at the Home Office concerning Peter's case.

She had been born Grace Parker in Buckinghamshire in 1903. She lived in a children's home very early in her life. In 1914 she was sent to Canada as a young emigrant. This was under one of the schemes to send 'deprived' children to the 'Dominions' [the independent countries such as Canada and Australia which were still members of the British Commonwealth.] Sadly for many these schemes were a path to worse deprivation and abuse.

Grace went to the Annie Macpherson Home in Stratford, Ontario. Later she married a Dutch-Canadian man, James Denike.[51] They had a son, James Parker Denike ('Jim'), born on 15 January 1926. Sadly, James Senior was killed in a car accident not long afterwards.

---

[51] Personal communication from Gillian Bulstrode, née Harrison, February 2016.

Following the death of her husband, Grace felt the call of home. In the summer of 1927, she and baby Jim embarked on the *SS Montclair* at Montreal, and headed for England. They landed at Liverpool on 19 August and moved to Leicester where they settled.

Six years later, in March 1933, Grace married Thomas Harrison, a postman. They were wed at the local registry office in Loughborough, and went on to make their home in that town, with James being brought up as a child of the family. The following year they were blessed with a son Thomas Robin ('Robin'). Two years later a daughter, Gillian, followed.

In 1938 tragedy struck. Robin, aged four, drowned following a fall into a canal. Jim had been fond of him, and was devastated. A year later, the wider calamity of war affected the whole world. Other problems now intervened. In 1942 Grace and Thomas separated. The children were to stay with Grace. She found it hard to find a new home which could accommodate all three of them.

Meanwhile, Jim - then working at the Brush Electrical Machines factory -was full of youthful exuberance. He seems to have been something of a handful, pestering his mother to allow him to join the army. Reluctantly, Grace gave her permission. Jim joined up in December 1942, a few weeks shy of his seventeenth birthday. Like Armin and so many others, he gave a false age – he purported to be almost eighteen.

Jim joined a Highland regiment, the Black Watch, although, as Gillian says 'we actually have no Scottish blood that I know of.' He seems to have revelled in the wearing of the tartan, although Gillian did not: 'I was greatly embarrassed when my brother came home on leave wearing a skirt!' Many who joined the army during the war did so by way of the Territorial Army (now the Army Reserve), so they could be swiftly released ('demobilised') at the end of hostilities. Jim, on the other hand, joined the regular army as he intended to make it his career even after the war ended.

The Black Watch were not due to go on operations abroad any time soon. However, another regiment in the Highland Division, the Gordon Highlanders, were due to do so. Jim had proved a good soldier – he was once first in a battalion cross-country run in full kit – and was eager to see action. He volunteered for a transfer to the Gordons, and this took effect in June 1943.

Meanwhile, Grace did find a new home – miles away in the West Country. Gillian remembers 'the lump in my throat when we left [Jim] in his army greatcoat outside the train that was to carry us down to Somerset and a new life.'

The long awaited invasion of the Continent occurred in the summer of 1944. Allied forces landed in Normandy. British, Canadian and American forces poured from southern England into the Normandy beachhead prior to an anticipated breakout. Jim went over to Normandy with his unit on 18 June, serving as a Bren gunner – the Bren being a light machine gun. On 26 June, British and Canadian forces, including the Gordon Highlanders, headed away from the coast towards Caen. Jim fell in action that very day in the bitter fighting around that town. He was buried temporarily in a corn-field. In due course Grace received a telegram stating that Jim was 'missing in action.'

Gillian recalls that her mother – maybe predictably – hoped that Jim had somehow survived. However, some time afterwards, a non-commissioned officer wrote to her to confirm Jim's death. Then and only then did she relinquish her hope 'that [Jim] had somehow got lost in the smoke of battle and was still alive.'

Afterwards, Gillian remembers her mother becoming cold and distant. She remembers that the confirmation of her brother's death had to come from someone other than her mother. It was reported in at least one Leicestershire paper, but Gillian might not have seen that as she lived far away by then.

The war ended the following year. Jim's body had been moved to the Commonwealth War Graves at St Manvieu Cemetary, Cheux. In time a headstone marked his resting place. In addition to the Gordon Highlanders' regimental crest, it carries Jim's full name, his correct age at death (18) and the haunting epitaph:

'All he had hoped for

All that he had, he gave.'

A year and some months after Jim's death, Grace wrote to support a reprieve for Peter. She signed herself 'Denike', rather than Parker or Harrison.

'17.10.45

The Home Secretary

London

Sir,

I am writing to you on behalf of Peter Jarmain, who has been sentenced to death for murder. I do not know the boy or anyone connected with him, I only know that he is 18, the same age as my own son, who died at Colleville, [near] Caen, fighting with his regiment.

No one can justify what Peter did, but believe me, at 18, a boy is still only a child and not old enough to be held wholly responsible for his actions. If we bring children up in an atmosphere of air raids and violence, teach them to extol and admire the taking of life (even in battle) then we should not hold them responsible to the point of hanging, for getting the wrong idea. I wish I could prove what I feel, that it was only the swing of his kilt and the tilt of his Balmoral which separated my son from this poor boy. It is my consolation that if I had kept my boy out of the army until he was older, he might have found an outlet for his undisciplined enthusiasm in just such an escapade as Peter.

Eighteen is so very young and so easily influenced. As I know from my memories of his last leave, squabbling with his 9 year old sister over the right to read the latest 'Rupert' annual first.

So, for the sake of my 18 year old boy and the thousands like him, please give this other 18 year old another chance. I am sure that tonight he is no hardened criminal, but only a frightened boy.

Yours respectfully

Grace Denike

> My son was No 14415092 P[riva]te James Parker Denike
>
The Gordon Highlanders.'

Jim Denike(Loughborough Roll of Honour website)

Grace Harrison(Gillian Bullstrode)

There was no time to waste. As before the appeal, plans were already afoot for Peter's execution if the Home Secretary decided not to grant a reprieve. Correspondence had already passed between the prison and the Home Office indicating that 1 November 1945 would be the date of the hanging, at Pentonville Prison.

Peter's fate was at least partly in his own hands. The Home Secretary would consider the case of anyone under sentence of death, whether they sought a reprieve or not. However, Peter put pen to paper to write the most important communication of his young life.

His petition is in the National Archives at Kew, in typed and handwritten versions.

The handwriting has been confirmed to be Peter's, but arguably some of the words may not be his. Perhaps the somewhat bombastic Basil St John Eagan had a hand in drafting it. At one stage he spells 'fantastic' as 'phantastic,' a very dated spelling even then.

In the petition Peter took the somewhat risky step of outlining a somewhat different account from that which was in his statement and in his evidence. One suspects this may have been the hand of Basil at work. It started, 'I respectfully request that this my Petition be considered, and that you will be pleased to review the sentence of death passed upon me by the judge [....]. Before all else I desire to tender my sincere sorrow for the unforgivable and incomprehensible behaviour which resulted in this terrible tragedy.'

In his account Peter explained how he was at the time of the crime 'in a thoroughly neurotic and unbalanced state of mind verging on the point of a nervous breakdown,' as a result of his unemployment. He referred to his disability, which, he said, had caused him to suffer an inferiority complex. Peter mentioned having been ridiculed by his employer, and giving up the job, not long before the crime. He had borrowed the money from Leonard's mother, but had no idea how he would pay it back. In this 'abnormal state of mind' he had gone to his local pub, or as he wrote, 'I resorted to the local Inn.' Implausibly he seemed to suggest that the idea of the robbery was put in his head by the soldier he met: 'I had the offer of a revolver from a soldier with the insinuation that I should use it to my advantage.'

He then went on to outline how the robbery occurred. Apparently he was walking along the road where the garage was, saw an unusual make of car, and stopped to look at it. He then noticed the garage office, and 'impulsively walked in.' He found a 'girl' counting money and took out the gun and asked her for the money. She told him not to be silly and to go away. He passed the gun from his left hand to his right and made a grab for the money. The 'girl' had stood up, and the gun 'for some unaccountable reason' went off. In this account Peter does not mention Ivy falling hurt, or groaning, nor does he even mention taking any of the money.

The petition ended in similar vein. Peter stated 'I swear before Almighty God that I never intended to take that poor girl's life,' and that he was 'fully alive to the fact that nothing he could do or say would ever restore her to life.' He went on to plead to the Home Secretary 'that a reprieve may be granted to me so that at some future time I may make restitution to those relatives who through my fault have been deprived of her support.' He made reference to his 'poor widowed mother,' and said of her : 'The faith of my mother has never wavered. The realisation of her love and unswerving loyalty has indeed helped me more than anything else to face up to the realities of my position.' He acknowledged that even a reprieve would mean 'many years of imprisonment,' and a punishment which 'can never cease.' Lastly he signed in the manner then used to end formal letters: 'I am, Sir, Your most respectful and obedient servant.'

In Kempton Park, Armin had likewise written another petition – dated 16 October

- and sent it to the confirming military authorities. The written petition seems not to have survived, but in it Armin apparently maintained his innocence. He also seems to have referred to two incidents before his captivity, in which, he said, he had provided blood for transfusion to wounded American soldiers, thus saving two lives.

It is not known whether Basil St John Eagan was granted an interview with the Home Secretary over Peter's case. In practice these meetings were generally held with the senior civil servants in the Home Office. At least one person did speak to the civil servants about Peter. A letter from Mr Mishcon's firm dated 26 October to the Under Secretary of State of the Home Office (the department's chief civil servant) makes this clear. The letter states that a petition signed by a number of local residents who knew Peter, had been put before the Home Office by Colonel Lipton, Member of Parliament for Brixton, who had recently visited the department.

The letter also referred to an offer of help from a less welcome source. A wealthy lady called Violet Van Der Elst was a prominent campaigner against capital punishment. She spent her considerable fortune standing as an independent candidate in parliamentary elections on that issue, invariably losing her deposit through insufficient votes. She would also protest on the morning of executions, often getting herself arrested in confrontations with the police. On one occasion in 1935 she had vans drive outside the prison playing the hymn 'Abide With Me,' while overhead three aeroplanes trailed banners reading 'Stop the Death Sentence.'[52] Apparently Peter's family had received repeated requests by Mrs Van Der Elst asking for her to be allowed to petition the Home Secretary on their behalf. The family were unwilling to allow Peter's case to be used by Mrs Van Der Elst. Probably, like others, they considered her something of an attention-seeker who would turn an execution from a solemn moment into an unseemly spectacle, if the worst happened.

---

[52] Lizzie Seal, *Law, Crime and History* (2013) p. 3.

Violet Van Der Elst (Grantham Matters website)

The letter ends, '[Any communication which you may receive from Mrs Van Der Elst is made without our client's instructions and knowledge.'

The Home Secretary – and the civil servants who gave him advice – followed a number of general principles in deciding capital cases. Such decisions were not entirely rule-based – popular opinion did play a part. In 1954, the senior civil servant at the Home Office wrote that

'The principles on which he decides what advice should be given to the [monarch] cannot be precisely defined. In some cases the decision is reasonably straightforward. The murderer may have committed a heinous and premeditated murder, and public opinion would be shocked by his reprieve; or on the other hand the prisoner may ....be a devoted mother who killed her imbecile child to save [them] from a life of misery, and public opinion would be equally shocked if the law were allowed to take its course.'[53]

Earlier still, a Home Secretary, speaking in the House of Commons, gave an explanation of the relevant considerations to be taken into account:

'Numerous considerations – the motive, the degree of premeditation or deliberation, the amount of provocation, the state of mind of the prisoner, his physical condition, his character and antecedents, the recommendation or absence of recom-

---

[53] *The Home Office*, by F A Newsam, George Allen and Unwin/OUP, 1954, page 115. The same source at page 116 states that in 1952, just under half of those sentenced to death for murder and not subsequently found insane, were reprieved.

mendation from the jury, and many others...'[54]

'Recommendation from the jury' referred to the practice by which a jury, although convicting a prisoner, could recommend to the judge that mercy should be shown. In murder cases, where the judge had no discretion in sentence, the judge would pass that on to the Home Secretary, who was in no way bound by it. The jury in Peter's case had made no such recommendation.

Another consideration – this time favouring Peter – was quite recent. In the early 1940s, the then Home Secretary, Herbert Morrison, decided in principle that eighteen-year olds convicted of murder would normally be reprieved, unless their crimes were particularly heinous.[55]

The task of deciding what advice would be given to the Home Secretary in Peter's case fell to Sir Frank Newsam. He

---

[54] Herbert Gladstone , HC Deb 11 April 1907 vol172 c366.

[55] FA Newsam, Home Office memorandum to Home Secretary, October 1945

was the Deputy Under-Secretary of State, the second most senior civil servant in the department. Newsam was born in Barbados, the son of a colonial civil servant stationed there. As a young man he had an impressive military career during and just after the First World War. He saw action in a number of campaigns, including the 1916 Easter Rising by Irish nationalists in Dublin. He had been awarded the Military Cross for his actions on the battlefields of the Western Front.

Sir Frank Newsam (Police Staff College, Bramshill)

After that war he joined the civil service and rose swiftly through its ranks. In 1941 he became Deputy Under Secretary in the Home Office. He was equally bold and decisive in putting forward advice to Home Secretaries in death penalty matters, as he had been on the battlefield. Later in 1945 he had to tender advice in the case of John Amery, the son of a cabinet minister and brother of a war hero. Amery had gone to Germany before the war, and made some broadcasts to Britain from there during the conflict. He had also taken part in a failed attempt to raise an SS unit from British prisoners of war. His treachery had not greatly affected his country at all, and there were some questions about his mental state. But Newsam was unflinching in his decision: if the self-confessed traitor Amery were reprieved, 'it would be difficult to convince the ordinary man that Amery had not received exceptional and privileged treatment.'[56] His advice was accepted by James Chuter Ede, the Home Secretary. The latter marked Amery's file with the fateful

---

[56] *Playboys and Mayfair Men: Crime, Class, Masculinity, and Fascism in 1930s London*' by Angus Mclaren.

words 'The law must take its course,' and Amery was duly hanged.

In Armin's case, the military commander sent the second petition to the Advocate General's department to consider whether it raised any legal objections to the proposed execution. The latter sent it back, indicating that there were no legal issues raised.

The commanding officer and the Advocate General's department were arguably playing ping-pong with a young man's life. The military justice system did not have the clear-cut distinctions the civilian system had, between the decider of guilt post-trial (the appeal court) and the decider of clemency (the Home Secretary). In the military the commander who had convened the court martial fulfilled both roles. In addition, the military at that time rarely found themselves in this situation.

This had not always been the case. It is well known that in the First World War the British military executed over three hundred men for desertion, cowardice and other such offences. What is not so well known is that far more were sentenced but not executed. Of three thousand men sentenced to death in that conflict, about three hundred and fifty were executed.[57] The overwhelming majority were reprieved. Thus the military at that time had a lot of experience in deciding whether mercy was appropriate. But by 1945, military executions were few and far between. This may explain why the officers who decided his case seem to have been concerned only with the guilt/innocence issue, or whether Armin was seventeen or eighteen at the time of his offence.

We can only speculate about what would have happened if Armin had been charged and tried before the civilian justice system. It is true that he might have come across to a jury as the fanatical Nazi he was. That may have turned them against him. But his extreme youth may have brought him some sympathy.

He and Emil Schmittendorf may also have benefitted from the English public's

[57] Major Gordon Corrigan, *Mud, Blood and Poppycock*, Cassell *2004*.

loathing of suspected treachery. The Englishman and Englishwoman speak critically of 'sneaks,' 'snitches' and 'grasses' and would probably have had little sympathy for Rettig. In addition, a jury may have included former prisoners of war or relatives of such, who would have understood the anger of prisoners against a comrade who betrayed an escape attempt.[58]   Hence a jury may well have acquitted Schmittendorf and Armin. Even had they been convicted, a jury may have recommended mercy as their crime, unlike the earlier murder of Rosterg, was arguably spontaneous and not premeditated. Armin would have had a better chance of a reprieve from the Home Secretary based on the practice set by Herbert Morrison. His true age would have become general knowledge, and sympathetic members of the public might have written on his behalf, as Grace did for Peter.

---

[58] During the war, British prisoners at the famous Colditz camp had proposed to hang a British man placed there by the Germans as an informant. The plan was only abandoned because 'no volunteer could be found to carry out the grisly task.' In the event the British prisoners simply asked the Germans to remove him from the camp which they did. 'The Quiet Man Of Thundersely Was The Colditz Traitor,' *Basildon, Canvey and Southend Echo*, 3 January 2008.

However, Armin's fate was in the hands of the London District's Commanding Officer, Brigadier Trappes-Lomax, who confirmed his conviction and death sentence. The young man, along with Emil Schmittendorf, was now merely awaiting the date of his execution.

Newsam's recommendation in Peter's case was made in a ten-page memorandum to the Home Secretary, dated the 24th of October. The first part contained a recital of the facts of the case, and of the arguments presented on Jarmain's behalf at the trial. He went on,

'It will be seen that in law the prisoner is guilty of murder, even on the view that he pressed the trigger of the revolver inadvertently while he was in the course of committing the crime of armed robbery. The only question, therefore, remaining is whether there are any extenuating circumstances which would justify a lenient view being taken of this case.'

Newsam related the facts of Peter's life up to the time of the crime. He referred to Peter's disability, and his determination to support his widowed mother. He alluded to a contention put forward on Peter's behalf, that he 'suffered from an inferiority complex owing to his physical condition and he "felt bound to prove to himself and to the outside world that he was a man".'

He then came to the factors which might provide mitigation. He outlined the rule set by the previous Home Secretary, and explained the application of the rule in the Cleft Chin case:

'Mr Morrison, when he was Home Secretary, adopted the policy that youth, in the case of persons under the age of 19 years, was a sufficient ground to justify the exercise of the prerogative of mercy, save in cases where the crime was of the most heinous nature and there were no other extenuating circumstances. It was in pursuance of this policy that Betty Jones, who was just over the age of 18 years, was reprieved, while her accomplice, the American soldier – Hulten – who was 23 years of age, was executed, although perhaps Betty Jones was the more depraved character of the two'.

In the memo, Newsam went on to outline further extenuating circumstances other that Peter's age. He stated the obvious, that only Peter was alive to say whether the shot was fired accidentally or otherwise. In any event, the possibility that it had been accidental was 'not inconceivable.' Going into the detail of the shooting, he went on:

'It is true that, having shot the deceased, he took no steps to come to her rescue or to call assistance, but proceeded [to complete] his crime. But this apparently callous behaviour may have been due to the fact that he lost his head and blindly carried out the intention with which he had entered the office.'

Overall, Sir Frank recommended mercy. There was, however a sting in the tail. In his last paragraph Newsam stated 'I think he should be held in prison for a prolonged period.'

His superior, the Under Secretary of State Sir Alexander Maxwell, scribbled his recommendations below.   After briefly referring to accidental nature of the shooting he wrote:

'This consideration together with the age of the prisoner (he is clearly a childish creature who is young even for 18) seems to me definitely to [lean in favour] of a reprieve.'

Below this were the handwritten comments of the final decision-maker, the Home Secretary James Chuter Ede. He wrote:

'A recommendation is to be made that the Royal Prerogative of mercy should be exercised and the sentence commuted to penal servitude for life.'

The Home Secretary's decision was dated 25 October 1945. It is not clear how soon this decision was communicated to Peter or his family. However, there followed a macabre twist which one can only hope was done inadvertently. It seems that on 29 October the Home Office put out an announcement that Peter's execution would take place on the following Thursday, that is the 1st of November. However, almost immediately afterwards came another announcement that he had been reprieved.[59]

Letters were sent to the various persons who had lobbied to save Peter's life, including Grace Harrison. She did not mention the episode to her daughter Gillian. The latter only learnt of her mother's role in Peter's case through the author's research.

---

[59] *Manchester Evening News* 29 October 1945.

Chapter Seven: 'A Happily Un-familiar Duty'

At Kempton Park, Armin – and his co-accused Emil Schmittendorf – would already have known that their petitions had been dismissed. The only thing delaying their hanging was that the military (unlike the civil authorities) needed the King's permission for it. Inevitably, this was a pure formality and it was duly granted.[60] On 15 November 1945, they were taken to a motor vehicle for transportation to Pentonville Prison, guarded by twelve military policemen. We do not know whether they were told that their executions were imminent. However, they would probably have been aware of the transfer of the previous five unfortunate prisoners to Pentonville a month earlier, so they would have had little doubt that their own time had come.

Both men were searched before they left Kempton Park, and on their arrival at Pentonville. Shortly after they reached Pentonville, they were taken to have their

---

[60] *Murder, Mutiny and the Military* by Gerry Rubin, previously cited.

heights measured and their weights noted. A memo from an officer of the London District command to the Deputy Provost Marshall (a senior officer of the military police) states chillingly that 'it is suggested that [the taking of the weights and measurements] might be done under the pretext of a medical inspection.' We shall see in due course what these details were needed for.

After the weighing and measuring, the Deputy Provost Marshall formally 'promulgated' the findings and sentence of the military court, that is he informed the prisoners of those decisions. He also informed them that their petitions had all been dismissed. Armin and Emil Schmittendorf were then led to their separate cells. They were guarded by the military policemen in shifts, two to each cell.

At four o'clock that afternoon, two German-speaking chaplains, one Roman Catholic and one Protestant, arrived at Pentonville to offer spiritual consolation to the two condemned men. Armin and Emil Schmittendorf were not allowed any visitors, but paper and pencils were made available for them to write any letters. It is not known whether either of them did.

Earlier, at about two o'clock that afternoon, two other men had arrived at the prison. Their task was not to provide any sort of consolation to the prisoners – far from it. Albert Pierrepoint and Alexander Riley had both travelled from Manchester. Pierrepoint was the lead executioner, and Riley was to be his assistant.

Theirs was a part-time occupation. They were employed by the Home Office on what would now be called a 'zero hours' contract. They were paid for training sessions that they had to undergo periodically. Otherwise they were paid for each 'job.' All executioners had other occupations – many were pub landlords. Riley was a scaffolder (the building kind), and Pierrepoint was a delivery driver. While they would probably not have met the prisoners, they may have watched them at exercise from behind a wall in the exercise yard.

The following morning, the newspapers published the first public confirmation that the men had been convicted at all. The

Manchester Guardian bore the headline 'Two Germans To Be Hanged.' Below was a story including the line, 'Two of the prisoners, Feldwebel Emil Schmittendorf and Gefreiter Armin Kuehne (sic), were found guilty [of murder] and sentenced to death. They will be hanged this morning at Pentonville Prison.'

Military rations had been brought into the prison for the military personnel and also the prisoners. On the previous day the condemned men had tea and supper, and on the morning of the execution they had breakfast. Presumably all these meals were of the same Spartan nature they would have been used to in prisoner-of-war camps.

As Pierrepoint only had one assistant, the executions were to take place separately, starting at nine o'clock the following morning. It is not known in which order they took place. Following accepted practice, Pierrepoint and Riley entered the cell of the first prisoner. The prisoner would have been in his cell, perhaps praying with the chaplain. The hangmen would have been followed by the usual execution party – the prison Governor, the medical officer for the prison and some prison officers. One of the prison officers would then slide a wardrobe or other item in the cell wall, which would reveal the room next door. Only then did the prisoner know that he had in fact been sleeping right next to the gallows. The prisoner saw, for the first and last time, the trapdoor, lever, cross-bar, and the noose.

The executioners pinioned the prisoner, securing his hands. He was brought to his feet and marched in to the room next door. The noose would then have been in position above the prisoner's head. He was made to stand on a chalk mark on the trapdoor beneath the noose.

The dapper Pierrepoint then whipped out what would have seemed to be a neatly folded pocket square from his suit jacket. It was in fact a white hood, which he then pulled over the prisoner's head.[61] After Riley secured the prisoner's ankles with a leather strap, Pierrepoint adjusted the noose around the prisoner's neck. Pierrepoint bent down and removed a safety pin

---

61   https://tarlton.law.utexas.edu/lifemasks

from the base of the lever. Standing up again, he swiftly pulled the lever and released the trap doors. The prisoner fell into the void below.

Here the measurements came into play. Hanging, using the method refined by British executioners over the previous century, was to kill the prisoner by breaking his or her neck rather than by strangulation as before. The lead executioner had to calculate the length of rope – the 'drop' – for each prisoner. This was done by looking at a 'table of drops' published by the Home Office, providing how much rope was to be given for varying heights and weights of prisoners. The hangman would adjust this for any fact known by him about the prisoner – whether the latter was of slight or muscular build for example. This sort of knowledge would usually have been gleaned by him from watching the prisoner at exercise the previous day.

The calculation of the drop was not an academic exercise. If too much rope was given, the prisoner might fall too far and be decapitated. If not enough was allowed, he or she would not fall far enough and would perish slowly by strangulation. The drops for the two prisoners varied greatly as did their build. The muscular Emil Schmittendorf weighted about fourteen stone (close to ninety kilograms) and was five feet ten inches tall (close to one hundred and seventy eight centimetres). He was given a drop of the same length as his height. Armin was much shorter, as we have seen, and weighed just under ten stone (about sixty three kilograms). His drop was eight feet, close to two-and-a half metres.

After the first prisoner was hanged, the prison medical officer went into the room below the gallows and examined the suspended prisoner, checking his heartbeat. While the hanging would have broken the prisoner's neck and severed the spinal cord causing brain death, the heart would continue to beat for several minutes. Thus the second execution would not take place until the first prisoner's heartbeat had stopped. The body would then be taken down. A new rope, calculated to the measurements of the second prisoner, was put in place. In due course, that prisoner followed his comrade into eternity.

Neither prisoner is mentioned in much detail in Pierrepoint's memoirs. The records of the prison and the military mention that restraints – body-belts, strait-jackets and so on – were available if needed, but there is no record of them being used. Hence it seems the men went peacefully to their deaths. The executioners then undressed the bodies, and wrapped them in shrouds awaiting post mortems.

Before their burial in the prison courtyard, an inquest was held on the two men. A coroner would have sat, with a jury. Sworn evidence would have been taken of the executioner, prison doctor and other parties. In each case, the verdict was given as 'judicial hanging.' Following the inquest death certificates were issued. Cause of death was given as 'dislocation of vertebrae'. Worryingly, Armin's age was recorded by the inquest as twenty-one, this is repeated in his death certificate and was the age released to the press.[62] Correspondence between the military and the prison authorities before his death made it clear that they knew that he was only eighteen.

Was this a mistake or a deliberate cover-up? As we have seen, the execution of eighteen-year olds was lawful – in fact the military could have put younger prisoners to death but chose not to. We shall probably never know why the age was wrongly stated. Someone must have either erroneously given his age at the inquest or written it down wrongly. Mistakes of course happen. But remembering the way Peter's age – and youthful appearance – swung sympathy behind him, it is just possible that the military authorities decided to publish Armin's 'official' age, knowing that this would make his death unremarkable. The execution of a very boyish-looking eighteen year old – even that of a recent enemy combatant – may have caused some public unease.

---

[62] Some recent works still give Armin's age as twenty-one – see *The Executioner's Bible* , by Steve Fielding, (John Blake) 2007, and *Churchill's Unexpected Guests* by Sophie Jackson previously cited.

Armin was one of four eighteen-year-olds to be hanged in the United Kingdom during the twentieth century, all but one at Pentonville. Pantry boy Henry Jacoby was hanged there in 1922 for the murder of an elderly female guest during a botched robbery at the hotel where he worked. In 1925, Arthur Bishop was executed, also at Pentonville, for the murder of the butler in a diplomat's town house where he, Bishop, had lately been employed. Lastly, Francis 'Flossie' Forsyth was hanged in 1960 for the murder of a young man in a robbery along a canal footpath. By then double executions were no longer carried out in the same place, so while his co-accused (twenty-three year old Norman Harris) was hanged at Pentonville, Forsyth was put to death at the same instant at Wandsworth prison. Armin was the only eighteen-year-old that Pierrepoint would ever hang.[63]

With a civilian execution, a notice would have gone up on the prison gates ear-

---

[63] In 1949 he executed James Farrell at Birmingham Prison for murdering a fourteen-year-old girl in the course of an attempted rape. Farrell had turned nineteen only days before his execution.

ly in the morning indicating that the execution of the named prisoner was to take place later on. After that it would be replaced by a notice stating that the prisoner had been executed. With the military execution of Armin and of Emil Schmittendorf, only the latter notice was posted.

Pierrepoint was paid £10 for the first execution, and a further £5 for the second. His assistant was paid £3, 3 shillings and £1, 11 shillings and 6 pence respectively.[64] Their travel expenses were also covered. Small sums were paid to the prison officers who assisted the military over the two days, to the prison doctor and to the workmen who built the coffins and buried the two prisoners. All told, the expenses of the executions amounted to just over £36 (worth about £1,100 now).

Days afterwards, the military authorities wrote to the prison staff to thank them for their cooperation in the October and November executions. In a letter dated 19 November the commanding officer London

---

[64] In pre-decimal money a shilling was one-twentieth of a pound, and six pence was one-fortieth.

District stated: '[T]he help and cooperation so willingly given was more than welcome to those of my officers whose task it was to arrange the carrying out of a happily unfamiliar duty.'

Chapter Eight: 'A Prolonged Period'

Just as King George VI had had a formal role in ending Armin's life, so he did in saving Peter's.

Above: Peter's conditional pardon. The King's signature is at top left. The Home Secretary's is at bottom right

A conditional pardon was issued by the monarch altering Peter's sentence from one of death to one of life imprisonment . Just as with the authorisation of Armin's execution, the King's role would follow advice from officials

It is said that 'when prisoners were reprieved, they often had to be transferred to the prison hospital for a time to recover from their emotional problems and shock before they could be put in the normal prison population.'[65]   This might explain why Peter remained at Wormwood Scrubs for about a month after his reprieve, although as a 'young offender' he would have to start serving his sentence in an appropriate prison.

In England and Wales, prisoners over eighteen were divided into two age categories – young offenders (aged between eighteen and twenty-one) and adult offenders (those over twenty-one). This distinction survives, even though for the last fifty years the age at which a person becomes adult has been eighteen instead of twenty-one. All those aged below twenty-one are normally kept separate from those above that age.   Peter, as an eighteen year old, was

[65] Capital Punishment UK website, and also see Chapter 13 of *A Fatal Pickup*, by Edna Gammon, Mereo Books 2015.

transferred to Camp Hill prison on the Isle of Wight, on 8 December 1945.

Peter's sentence was one of 'penal servitude.' Historically, prisoners had been sentenced to imprisonment with or without hard labour, or to penal servitude. Penal servitude was meant to be a more severe form of imprisonment with hard labour, and had been created as a replacement for transportation to the Australian colonies. However, even by 1945, the difference between all these classes of detention was disappearing. The familiar mental image of prisoners breaking rocks on a moor was already outdated.

After less than a year at Camp Hill, and still as a young offender, Peter was transferred in October 1946. This time he went much further north, to the prison at Wakefield in Yorkshire. This is much further from London than the Isle of Wight is, and it may well be that it was harder for his family to visit him there. He was to spend two years there. Wakefield is a severe, forbidding building, still in use as a maximum security prison. There has been a prison on the site since the sixteenth century.

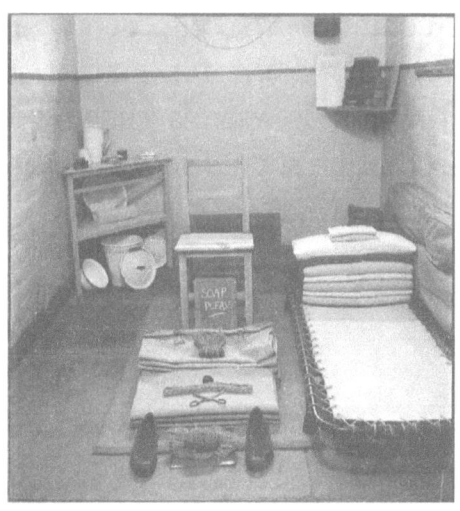

A prisoner's kit laid out for inspection, HMP Wakefield, 1944. (Imperial War Museum)

A memo from the Governor later described him as having been on arrival 'surly and anti-social.' The memo continues - perhaps harshly - that this was 'due to the upbringing thrust on him by a silly, doting, and possessive mother.'

Peter was enrolled in various courses to help him learn useful skills. Only a few months after his arrival at Wakefield, Peter seemed to have had enough of prison life. He petitioned the Home Secretary, this time seeking an early release to join the army. This was always an unlikely request. Peter's medical condition was almost certainly going to rule him unfit for military service. Also, Sir Frank Newsam's recommendation had been that he should serve a long time in prison.

Workshop at HMP Wakefield,1944 (Imperial War Museum)

In this petition, dated 8 January 1947, Peter wrote that he 'was making full use of the educational facilities provided by [the] prison to better myself and [my] habits for my future entry into the social world [,] also my release would be beneficial to society and my country by my enlisting in the armed forces.' He also wrote that he 'now realise[d] the full seriousness of my crime and I am doing everything in my power to atone [for] it.'

A reply was a long time coming. Perhaps Peter feared that his petition had been lost in the system, perhaps he got his hopes up at the time being taken to consider it, perhaps both. In the event there was to be no good news for him. On 20 February 1947, the Home Office directed the prison governor to inform Peter that the Home Secretary 'is unable to accede to your request that a date be fixed for your release.'

Peter's behaviour was generally satisfactory. By autumn of 1947 he was being considered for transfer to the adult programme. This was seen as a promotion, one which could see him in an open prison. However he seems to have been guilty of some disciplinary offence, on which the record is terse. In the words of the prison memo previously quoted 'he had a silly outburst of childishness and spoilt his record. He apologised for this and I think it taught him a lesson, as he took punishment well.' Elsewhere, his records show that he lost three days of remission during his time in prison, possibly as a result of this offence. He remained at Wakefield for another year. His twenty-first birthday found him there, still in the youth programme.

In the memo referred to above the Governor went on, 'Jarmain is definitely growing up. He possesses a lot of decent instincts, and should develop into a decent citizen. He is however, a weak youth [...],.. [q]uiet and introspective...easily led, credulous and somewhat naïve.' The Governor also said '[Peter] is no leader; I doubt if he will ever become one.' Around this same time Peter was examined by a prison psychotherapist, who stated that Peter 'appears to be developing self-knowledge and control in normal manner,' and did not require psychotherapy.

Peter was transferred to HMP Leyhill in Gloucestershire, an open prison, as an adult, in early 1949. Later that year reports were drawn up recording his progress or otherwise in his first four years in custody. These were compiled in three parts – one each written by the prison doctor, chaplain and governor.

The doctor reported that Peter was in good health, and that there was no evidence of any bad effects caused by imprisonment. He noted that Peter had gained about a stone in weight (approximately 6.35 kilograms) since his conviction, and now weighed a little over ten stone (about sixty-three kilograms). The governor noted that he was 'still very much a child,' though he had settled down and [was] working very well.' The chaplain stated that Peter was 'rather a weak man and easily led. He likes to be popular'. All three reported that Peter was working satisfactorily – at various courses and also in the garden.

Peter received regular visits from his family members, as was noted by the prison authorities. He would have been kept up to date on developments outside. His sister Betty had married Reginald Charles Dix, a soldier, in January 1946. She had finally been demobilised that December. The following March, Emily Jarmain remarried, to Arthur Cope, also widowed.

In May 1951, Victor Mishcon wrote to the Home Office on Emily's behalf asking them to consider releasing Peter. The Home Office wrote back indicating that 'it may be some considerable time yet before he is prepared to agree to Jarmain's release'. Internal Home Office memoranda referred to the fact that Sir Frank Newsam had recommended that Peter serve a lengthy period of custody. In addition, other memoranda indicate that the average period served by reprieved murderers was eight years, and therefore Peter could not expect to be released until such a period had expired, or even later.

While Peter may have settled down into prison life, he was still determined to secure his release as soon as possible. In November 1952 he wrote to the Home Secretary again. 'I have now completed over seven years' imprisonment,' he wrote, 'and now feel confident and competent to earn my living and take my place in the outside world as a useful citizen.' He stated that he had done a vocational training course in painting and decorating, and gained a City and Guilds intermediate certificate. He continued, 'I feel sure of getting suitable employment where I can put the knowledge gained to suitable advantage.' Once again, his request did not receive an immediate reply. Christmas brought a response – but not a festive one. The Home Office's reply stated that the Home Secretary 'has considered your petition...but is not yet prepared to fix a date for your release.'

A second four-year report on Peter, in autumn of 1953, seemed to show progress. The doctor confirmed that Peter was in fairly good health although 'not very robust physique.' Peter had been 'employed on the lighter forms of work' and 'excused violent exercises and games,' due to his health. He was cheerful and cooperative, and prison seemed not to have been harmful to him physically or mentally. The chaplain said that there had been 'a marked improvement' in Peter since his arrival, and that he had become 'more stable and mature.' The Governor reported that Peter had been appointed a leader that March, thus disproving the pessimistic predictions of the Wakefield governor some years before. This was seen as 'a fitting reward for his efforts to cooperate in his training and his anxiety to help in the voluntary activities' in the prison. Peter was training as a painter and decorator, for which work he was 'well qualified' in the Governor's opinion.

The Brixton MP, Colonel Lipton, who had taken part in the campaign to spare Peter's life, was still involved in the case, writing to the Home Office in August 1953. This seems to have triggered a burst of official activity. An internal Home Office memo dated 2nd October indicated that Peter was ready for release, stating among other things 'It is thought that further detention may act adversely on the improvement achieved in his character.' In October 1953, a junior Home Office minister wrote to Lipton in reply to the MPs letter from August on behalf of 'Mrs Pope' (obviously a misspelling of 'Cope'). The minister stated that 'the Home Secretary has carefully reviewed the circumstances of Jarmain's case and he has decided that he may be released on licence in September 1954, subject to his continued good conduct.' Another letter in similar terms was addressed to the prison governor at Leyhill, advising him to inform Peter of this decision.

In June 1954, Peter spent a period of home leave with his family. According to a memo from the Governor to the Prison Commissioners dated 30 July, 'he appears to have benefitted from the brief spell of freedom.' In the same memo it was said that Peter 'continued to behave in an exemplary manner,' and also '[maintained] his interests in classes, sports and amateur theatricals.'

The Home Secretary was satisfied that the time had come for Peter to be released. On 28 August 1954 the Home Office issued a licence stating that he was to be released within fifteen days. However it contained the warning that he was liable, for the rest of his life, to be recalled by the Home Secretary.

On 11 September 1954, Peter was released. In the years since he had been imprisoned, Britain had gained a new monarch, Queen Elizabeth II, and had fought three years of war in Korea. The Conservatives had returned to power, and Winston Churchill was back at 10 Downing Street. Television broadcasting, suspended at the outbreak of war, had returned, and increased hugely in popularity after the Queen's televised coronation. Food rationing had ended in June. Rock and roll music and teen culture were taking root. Peter stepped out into a bold new world.

Chapter Nine: Aftermath

After his release, Peter was assisted in his resettlement by being placed at a factory in London. He took part in amateur dramatics and variety shows there, no doubt building on his experience at Leyhill. At the factory he met a younger woman working there. They started going out, and Peter quickly disclosed his recent history. The woman was not put off by this, and the relationship continued. They married in 1958, and went on to have two sons and a daughter.

Peter and his family made their home in Kent. He spent most of his life working as a painter and decorator, and sign-painter. Later he found work as an electro-plater. He was a much-loved father and in time, grandfather. He never lost the love for headgear – many of his post-release pictures show him wearing hats or with them near him. He repaid the Home Secretary's trust, never getting into trouble with the law again.

His mother, Emily , now widowed again, passed away in 1971. Of the siblings who featured in this account, his sister Betty died in 1991, and brother Sydney in 2002.

Sadly Peter was struck down suddenly by a terminal illness in the summer of 1996, dying in a hospice at the age of sixty-nine. He and his wife had always planned to share his history with their children, but the time never seemed right. Finally, the illness carried him off before he had the chance. The children (now of course grown-up) learned the secret some years after Peter died.

Ronald Samuel Booth passed away on 30 June 1953, aged fifty. He seems not to have been living with his wife at the time. His address – also the place of his death - was given as 30 Thornton Road, the premises next door to the garage. His estate totalled over £10,000.00 - over a quarter of a million pounds in today's money.

Ivy's brother H____, married in July 1946, to a young lady in her mid-twenties. They do not appear to have had any children. H_____ died in 1990. His widow was still alive when the author was researching this book a few years ago. She did not reply to requests for assistance with the enquiries.

Edward Phillips remarried in the summer of 1946, at a Roman Catholic church in Blackpool. His bride was a nurse in her mid-twenties, her surname indicating Belgian or French origins. Perhaps he had met her while working at the military hospital in Brussels. One of the witnesses was one 'Kenneth Wolstenholme,' possibly the then bomber pilot later to become a famous television sports broadcaster, whose 'they think it's all over' World Cup commentary in 1966 is still fondly remembered (in England at least). Edward was to have a son and daughter by his second wife. Sadly, he passed away in 1969, aged only fifty-one. It appears that Edward's children did not learn of his first marriage until after his death.

Peter's friend Lennie Dunn passed away in 1994. Donald Caston has proved more elusive – just as he was in 1945 when he gave first the military authorities, then the civil police, the slip. The author has traced him to his native Norfolk in the early

1970s, where he seems to have married, but there the trail goes cold. If still alive now, Donald would be in his mid-nineties, and perhaps the last surviving major witness from Peter's trial. Strangely, his real name is blacked out of the police file but not that of the Prison Commissioners.

Inspector Bastable retired shortly after Peter's reprieve. He died in 1972, incidentally at Mayday Hospital, where Ivy had breathed her last twenty-seven years earlier. His death certificate only refers to his previous occupation as a policeman, so there is no indication of any career he may have pursued after retirement.

Grace Harrison died in 1986, aged about 83.

Laurence Byrne was made a High Court judge in November 1945. He was to gain fame as the trial judge when the publishers of the DH Lawrence book 'Lady Chatterley's Lover' were tried for obscenity in 1960, and acquitted. This was his last trial before his retirement, and he died five years later.

His adversary, Frederick Lawton, stayed at the bar for longer. He became a Queen's Counsel (a senior barrister or 'silk') in 1957. His pupil barristers included Robin Day, who became a famous television presenter, and Margaret Thatcher, later a politician and Britain's first woman prime minister.   Lawton became a High Court judge in 1961, and was raised to the Court of Appeal eleven years later. He presided over some famous trials, including the second murder trial of the gangster Kray brothers, and later that of their rival Charlie Richardson. Sir Frederick Lawton died in 2001, thus outliving his young client from 1945.

Sir Frank Newsam became the head civil servant at the Home Office three years after dealing with Peter's case. He held that position until 1957. He developed an interest in policing, founding the Police Staff College at Bramshill. The picture of him in this book is on display at that college. Newsam died in 1964.

Victor Mishcon continued his legal practice. His firm had the distinction of having acted for two tragic twentieth- century women in their divorces – Diana Princess of Wales, and Ruth Ellis. The Princess needs no further mention. Ellis was a nightclub hostess who divorced her husband and later had a relationship with racing driver David Blakely, who was abusive towards her. In 1955, after they split up, she confronted him with a revolver and shot him dead. She was tried, convicted and sentenced to death. Mishcon made representations to the Home Secretary to spare her life, as he had with Peter. This time there was to be no reprieve, and Ellis became the last woman to be hanged in Britain. His firm became Mishcon de Reya following a 1988 merger. Mishcon continued his political career, becoming a Labour Party peer, and later shadow Lord Chancellor. He died in 2006.

The 'felony murder' rule, under which Peter was convicted, was abolished in England and Wales in 1957. Afterwards, an accidental killing during robbery or rape would be manslaughter not murder. The change in the law came into play in the 1967 trial of a British soldier for the killing of a taxi driver in Osnabruck in Germany. The soldier, Leslie Grantham, claimed to have accidentally shot the driver during a bungled robbery. If this defence had succeeded , he would have been convicted of manslaughter. However he was not believed and was convicted of murder by a British court. He served ten years of a life sentence. Like Peter, he ended his sentence at Leyhill, where he also took part in amateur dramatics. Afterwards, Grantham took up acting professionally, playing the part of the villainous 'Dirty Den' Watts in the TV soap opera *Eastenders*.[66]

The rule survives in New South Wales in Australia, in Trinidad and Tobago and elsewhere in the West Indies, and in Sierra Leone and elsewhere in Africa. An even wider version of it exists in some states of the US. There, if three commit a bank robbery and one is shot dead by the police, the surviving robbers can be tried for the murder of their companion.[67]

---

[66] *Metro* 15 June 2018.

[67] 'If He Didn't Kill Anyone, Why Is It Murder?' *New York Times* June 27 2018.

Albert Pierrepoint, who hanged Armin and who would probably have dispatched Peter if the latter had not been reprieved, retired as an executioner in 1956. By then he had been a pub landlord for some years. His Oldham pub was called 'Help The Poor Struggler,' but was nicknamed 'Help The Poor Strangler.' In 1951, Pierrepoint had to hang a regular customer at his pub, James Corbitt, for the murder of his, Corbitt's, girlfriend. Years before his death in 1992, he published his memoirs. In them, he contended that the death penalty did not serve as a deterrent:

'There have been murders since the beginning of time, and we shall go on looking for deterrents until the end of time. If death were a deterrent, I might be expected to know. It is I who have faced them last, young lads and girls, working men, grandmothers. I have been amazed to see the courage with which they take that walk into the unknown. It did not deter them then, and it had not deterred them when they committed what they were convicted for. All the men and women whom I have faced at that final moment convince me that in what I have done I have not prevented a single murder.'[68]

German prisoners of war in Britain were to remain there for up to two years more, being used as a source of labour. The author does not know at what stage Armin's family found out about his death. As we have seen they had fallen behind the Iron Curtain, the division between communist and non-communist Europe. News from the West may have been in short supply.

Tragedy persisted for the Kuhne family – in 1947 another son, Gunter, passed away, the third of the boys to die aged eighteen. In an ironic twist on the pre-war relationship between the couple, Armin's mother went on to have an affair, having two children as a result. The marriage broke down, and Armin's father came to West Germany. He died there years later, in 1957. It is known that he had served a spell in prison not long before his death, although it

---

[68] *Executioner, Pierrepoint,* 1974.

is not clear what for.[69]   His mother remained in the East, where she passed away
in 1989, as the communist regime was
crumbling.

Armin, Emil and the Comrie murderers lie under the courtyard of Pentonville
Prison to this day. Following the abolition of
capital punishment in mainland Britain in
1965 the Home Office allowed the bodies of
hanged persons to be removed to be reburied elsewhere – this is true whether or not
they have been exonerated of their alleged
crimes. Some from outside Britain have has
their remains sent home – such as Roger
Casement (reburied in Ireland) and Udham
Singh (cremated on the return of his remains to India). Both had been executed
and initially buried at Pentonville. The
German government has not moved the remains of Armin and the others. Meanwhile,
most of Germany's war dead who perished
in or near Britain are buried in a cemetery
at Cannock Chase, in Staffordshire. Rosterg
and Rettig, the men who were killed as supposed traitors, are buried there. The men

---

[69] Personal communication from Marco Mundhenk, late
2018.

who killed them – supposedly in the name of Germany - lie in felons' graves.

Lastly, the crime scene of the Red Arrow murder remains in the motor trade. The picture below shows how it looks now. The site of Lodge Moor Camp, near Sheffield, the location of Rettig's murder, is not now in use. It was recently the subject of an archaeological dig to unearth its wartime history. [70]

Garage at Thornton Road, pictured in 2015 (Conrad Lisk)

---

[70] UK's biggest second world war prisoner camp unearthed in Yorkshire.'*The Guardian* 4 July 2019]

Postscript

As the law which secured Peter's conviction is no longer in force in England, his case is better known beyond these shores. It was in a Commonwealth university that I first learnt of it. One of the books I read there was F T Giles's *The Criminal Law*[71] where Peter's case is alluded to, thus:

'Jarmain confronted a woman cashier with a pistol, and called upon her to hand over what money she had. She refused. Jarmain showed her that the pistol was loaded. He transferred it to his left hand and it went off. The woman received injuries from which she later died. He was convicted.'

Reading various textbooks while doing my law degree there, I pondered the result whereby a man was (I thought) hanged for a crime which he had arguably not intended. Ivy was often referred to in the books as a 'girl', rather than the very mature woman she was. Peter's age was not alluded to. I

---

[71] (1954), Pelican, p 189.

pictured him as a career villain, and Ivy as a teenager or not much older. A few years later, I read a casebook which contained printed the judgement in Peter's case, with a note below stating 'Jarmain was not executed.' That intrigued me, and I developed an interest in the case.

I lived in Thornton Heath, Croydon, for a few years. After I moved away from there that I started to research the case, and was surprised to find out that the crime had taken place a short walk from where I had lived. The research took me many years. I was pleased to make contact with relatives of the convicted teenagers, Armin and Peter, and with a relative of Jim Denike. However I was disappointed not to be able to contact any relatives of Ivy or of Ronald Booth, or anyone connected with them. Limitations of resources and language meant that I was not able to contact any relatives of the other German prisoners of war, defendants or victims.

My reflections on the cases:

I feel great sorrow for Ivy. Her son died young, her marriage failed, and her relationship with Ronald may have been on the wane as well. She bravely served her community during the Blitz, resisted an armed robbery, and fought in vain to recover from her wound. I have not been able to find out where she was buried or cremated. She left no relatives that I know of.

This book serves as a memorial to her.

We shall never know whether Peter pulled the trigger deliberately. For my part I believe he did not. His accounts of the shooting were remarkably consistent. I feel that he was seduced by the glamorous gangsters of book and film, and maybe fell for the 'tall tales' that his friends in uniform may have told. Owing to his disability he would never serve in the military. He most likely knew that Donald Caston was a deserter, and may have been attracted by the idea of law-breaking and defying authority. He probably felt that by carrying out the robbery he would 'prove himself'. He not only never killed again but never committed any other crime. He took the chance given to him by the Home Secretary.

Peter's children, grandchildren and now great-grandchildren are his memorial. He never forgot the crime which could have cost him his life. And it was only his own early demise that prevented him from sharing this with his children.

Two other eighteen-year-olds did not get second chances in life. Jim Denike died in action, breaking his mother's heart. However she lobbied for Peter's life, and no doubt saw the reprieve as a sort of 'resurrection by proxy', as her daughter Gillian puts it.

Armin did not get a reprieve. We will never now know what would have become of him in later life, had he lived. Some books state that he was a fanatical Nazi to the last. This may not be accurate. His last known letter, in which he says 'It has to be. HEIL YOU. Death sentence,' was written just after his conviction and months before his death. As the truth of defeat became accepted, and the horrors of the concentration camps became public, many of the Nazi prisoners lost their fanaticism. Others retained it and became Neo-Nazis later on.

Armin never got to choose between those paths.

Whatever the rights and wrongs of punishing people who saw themselves as dealing with treachery, it may be felt that Armin perhaps deserved a reprieve. In addition to his age, he had lived almost all his life under Nazism and knew no other system of values.

Rettig was also unfortunate. By most accounts he had not been an informer. He was literally in the wrong place at the wrong time, a non-Nazi in a mostly Nazi camp. He was a professional soldier, who had either never been fond of the Party or had grown disillusioned with it. The bungled attempt to move him sealed his fate. However, his sacrifice is honoured by his country, and he lies with his nation's war dead at Cannock Chase.

Rettig's grave at Cannock Chase. Another, unrelated, soldier is commemorated there too (Emma Crutchley)

Prisons in the mid-twentieth century seemed to work quite hard to rehabilitate prisoners. Rather than just being thrown inside to rot, Peter learnt a trade. The prisons back then were not overly austere or harsh for their own sake – the picture of a Wakefield cell shows this. Also of note is the brevity of the sentences served by murderers then (albeit most had suffered the terror of anticipating an early death by hanging). These days, when many complain that killers 'only serve a few years,' it is of note that today's murderers serve far longer than the eight-year average spoken of in the Home Office papers. An eighteen year old who shot someone fatally in a robbery today – whether convicted of murder or manslaughter – would serve far more than nine years. And probably in more overcrowded prisons than Peter served his time in.

As I concluded this manuscript, the UK was pondering whether to allow another fanatical teenager, nineteen year old Shamima Begum,[72] back into the country following her stay in the territory controlled by the so-called 'Islamic State' group in the Middle East. And other teenagers, eager to show their maturity, carry knives on city streets with tragic results. Sadly, there are youths today seeking to follow the criminal; paths that Armins and Peter took.

We can only hope that the lessons of the past are learned by today's youths, and that cycles of violence and fanaticism can come to an end.

The End

---

[72] 'I regret everything and I was brainwashed…give me a second chance,' *Evening Standard* 1 April 2019.

With Violent Hands

With Violent Hands

With Violent Hands

www.ingramcontent.com/pod-product-compliance
Lightning Source LLC
Chambersburg PA
CBHW022203170626
46807CB00005B/2330